Previously published Worldwide Suspense titles by
PAUL CARR

LONG WAY DOWN
THE CAYMAN SWITCH
THE BLACK PALMETTO
BAD WAY OUT
DEAD MAN'S TAKE

DEAD MAN'S GAME

PAUL CARR

W🌐RLDWIDE

TORONTO • NEW YORK • LONDON
AMSTERDAM • PARIS • SYDNEY • HAMBURG
STOCKHOLM • ATHENS • TOKYO • MILAN
MADRID • WARSAW • BUDAPEST • AUCKLAND

WORLDWIDE™

Recycling programs
for this product may
not exist in your area.

ISBN-13: 978-1-335-47503-9

Dead Man's Game

First published in 2019 by Paul Carr.
This edition published in 2022.

Copyright © 2019 by Paul Carr

For questions and comments about the quality of this book,
please contact us at CustomerService@Harlequin.com.

Harlequin Enterprises ULC
22 Adelaide St. West, 41st Floor
Toronto, Ontario M5H 4E3, Canada
www.ReaderService.com

Printed in U.S.A.

DEAD MAN'S
GAME

ONE

SHERIFF'S CRUISERS LINED the winding driveway of the Key West estate. Michael Dalton held up his badge for a deputy standing guard at the street. When he got the nod, he double-parked near the marble steps of the Mediterranean portico. He spotted a security camera under the eave as he entered.

Life-sized statues of bathing nudes stood inside a gurgling fountain in the expansive entrance hall. A deputy glanced at his badge and said, "They're in the bedroom, all the way down on the left." Dalton stretched on vinyl gloves and booties from boxes waiting on a table next to the door.

The body of a man lay on the floor at the foot of the bed, his eyes staring at the far wall. Dalton glanced that way, in case there was something there worth seeing. There wasn't. A red indention the size of a dime rested in the victim's forehead, an inch or so above his right eye. Blood had soaked a spot in the carpet the size of a dinner plate, and spattered the bed and the wall behind it. No shell casing in sight. The killer had used a revolver or picked up the brass. The victim had shoulder-length blonde hair, and appeared not to have shaved in a couple of days, the beard a shade of red and speckled with gray. He had bruises and cuts on his cheek and lips.

A man wearing a CSI vest photographed the scene, the muffled pop of the strobe the only noise in the room.

A dresser with a mirrored surface sat a few feet away. Atop it lay a heap of white powder, flanked by four cut rows and a gold inhaling straw. Somebody had interrupted a cocaine binge. Dalton glanced at the victim. A dust of the powder surrounded his nostrils. He wore a sneer on his face, maybe irked that he had enjoyed his last snort.

A deputy carrying a clipboard stepped over. His nametag read *Rob Daniels*. He said, "Who're you?"

"Michael Dalton. I transferred in a few weeks ago."

"Yeah, I heard about you. You're the one who caught the killer of those four Islamorada men a few months ago."

"That seems to follow me around." The murders had been fallout from the heist of a crime lord's $5 million cash hoard. Dalton's name had been in the news a lot as the case progressed.

"Good. We need somebody who can close a case." He grinned. "But don't tell anybody I said that. Key West PD just left. The officer said this is outside their jurisdiction, which I already knew."

"Any ID yet?" Dalton asked, nodding toward the man on the floor.

Daniels raised an eyebrow. "You don't know who this is?"

"No. Should I?"

Shrugging, Daniels said, "He's a Key West celebrity. Riley Gunn. Bad-boy vocalist for the rock group Redgunn."

Dalton glanced at the dead man. "Huh. He lives here?"

"Yeah. He bought this place less than a year ago, and has already ticked off a bunch of people."

"How so?"

"Wild parties, loud music, other stuff. Key Westers are pretty tolerant, but they do want some peace and quiet occasionally. He had a party last night, and we got a couple of calls about the noise."

"Who found him?" Dalton asked.

"The housekeeper called it in. I told her to wait in the dining room 'til we looked the place over."

"You find a phone?"

"No. We looked for that first. The killer might've taken it with him." He turned toward the hallway. "The ME is coming in now. Have you met him?"

"No, I haven't."

"Okay, come on over and I'll introduce you."

A small man with thinning hair and a mustache stepped into the room. Two assistants followed behind him with a gurney.

"Dr. Bragg, this is Detective Dalton. He's new, came in from Islamorada."

Dalton nodded. The ME eyed him up and down without a word, pursed his lips, and then turned and eased over to the body. Daniels followed and told him what he knew about the victim as Dalton headed out the door.

The housekeeper sat in the dining room, her arms on the table, hands clenched together. She was young, no more than twenty five, and attractive. No uniform or apron. Tears trailed down the sides of her face, maybe because her boss had been killed, or her job had come to an end. Or maybe her relationship was more than that of a housekeeper.

"I'm Detective Dalton with the Monroe County Sheriff's Office. I understand you found the body."

The woman nodded. "Yes, that is right." She had a slight accent.

He took out his notepad and sat down across the table from her. "Can I get your name?"

"Ana Kovich."

"All right, Ana, tell me how you found him."

She glanced in the direction of Gunn's bedroom. "His door was closed. I thought he was sleeping. He asked me to wake him up at eight because he had a meeting in town at nine. I knocked on the door, but he didn't answer, so I opened it and there he was on the floor." She put her head in her hands and sobbed.

"I understand he had a party last night."

After a few seconds, she dabbed her face with a tissue and nodded. "Yes, he did."

"Were you there, at the party?"

Shaking her head, she said, "I left after fixing the drinks and food, about 9:00."

"Who were the guests?"

"Mostly his band members and their guests."

"Can you give me their names?"

Her eyes narrowed. "I don't know them all."

"All right, give me the ones you know."

Ana went over the list and Dalton wrote them down. Two were band members, and she knew the names of two women who came with them. Another woman, mid-forties and blonde, also attended, but Ana didn't know her name or anything about her. The two remaining guests, both men, were unknown to her. Dalton thought he might get the information from the other guests.

"You live here?" Dalton asked.

"No, I have my own place."

"Can you think of a reason why any of the guests might've entered Mr. Gunn's bedroom?"

Frowning, she said, "I don't know. I didn't see anybody go back there. They were all in the living room when I left."

"Did you notice any sign of an argument or disagreement?"

"Noooo. They were all laughing and joking around."

Dalton leaned back in his chair and stared for a moment. The partiers might have been having a good time, but something went wrong at some point. "Does Mr. Gunn keep any cash or valuables in the house?"

She pursed her lips, as if thinking, then said, "He has a safe. I don't know what he keeps in it. It's in his bedroom in the closet." He made a mental note to check it out.

"Okay, do you know of anyone who might want Mr. Gunn dead?"

She glanced down at her hands and then dropped them to her lap. "Umm, no, I don't think so."

"You sure?"

After a pause, she said, "He could be abrasive, but most people liked him."

"Did they like him, or like what he could do for them?"

Ana frowned again. "Maybe both."

"How long have you worked for him?"

"Thirteen months. He hired me when he moved here."

Dalton got a phone number and told her she could leave. He walked through the house, but didn't see anything of interest. Four other bedrooms looked as if no one had ever used them. Maybe Gunn didn't invite guests to stay over. No office. No security system, either. Maybe a company managed the camera he had seen out front.

As he returned to the master bedroom, the ME's staff loaded the body onto the gurney. Deputy Daniels spotted him and stepped over. "The ME won't know a time of death or the caliber of the weapon until later. I told him to send you the information."

Nodding, Dalton said, "Which of the CSIs is in charge?"

The deputy pointed out the tall guy with the camera. "His name is Lucas Tarver."

"Bring him over."

The deputy did as he asked and Dalton said, "Several people attended a party here last night, and the killer could've been one of them. I want you to dust the living room and the bathrooms." Tarver winced, but nodded. "I might need to come back later," Dalton said to Daniels, "so seal this place up and post a deputy at the street to keep everybody out. That includes anybody from the news media."

"Roger that."

"Have your guys talk to the neighbors to see if they heard or saw anything suspicious, and if they have any security cameras that might shed any light on the shooting."

When Daniels headed for the door, Dalton spotted an alcove in the corner and stepped over. He found a large closet inside. A safe sat on the floor against the back wall, its door ajar. Stooping, he swung it open and peered inside at the empty chamber.

DALTON SHARED A two-person cubicle with his partner, Buddy Crook, who met him as he entered. Crook, a tall thin man, had been a deputy for nearly thirty years. He wore his scraggly, dyed brown hair down over his collar.

"Hey, thanks for covering for me this morning," Crook said.

"You bet." Dalton had gotten the call from Lt. Springer as he went out the door of the cottage where he lived at his uncle's marina. Springer said he couldn't get in touch with Buddy.

"The LT caught me on the way in a half-hour ago," Crook said, his voice pitched higher than normal. "He didn't look too happy about me not being there to help you."

"Don't worry about it, Buddy. I got what we needed."

The lieutenant had briefed him before assigning Crook as his partner: "Buddy's a good guy, but he's a little past his prime. He plays guitar in a band, and I get the impression he's a lot more interested in that than in police work. He likes the computer, though, so you can use him for research." Music to Dalton's ears.

Dalton told him who got murdered.

"You gotta be kidding! Riley Gunn is dead?"

"Shot in the head. Had a pile of blow on his dresser."

Buddy shook his head. "Sad. Dude stopped in at the club one night while we were playing a set. Him and two others. They looked drunk out of their minds, and they never gave us a second glance."

"He had a party last night. Seven people were there, and one of them could've shot him." Dalton tore the page of names from his notepad and handed it to him. "How about researching these? Also, find out who handles Gunn's security system. He had a camera out front, but I didn't notice any hardware in the house. I'm going in to brief Springer." He started to leave, but turned back. "Oh, yeah. They didn't find a phone. See if you can track down Gunn's carrier and get his recent call history."

Crook scribbled notes on a sheet of paper. "You got it, brother."

Dalton stepped down the hall to get a cup of coffee from the break room. Lt. Springer came out as he headed in. "Just coming to tell you about the case," Dalton said.

"Good," Springer said. "The sheriff will be there in a couple of minutes. Kill two birds."

A few minutes later, Dalton entered the lieutenant's office and sat at a conference table with him and Sheriff Thomas Diaz. A former detective from Miami, Diaz had worked with Dalton on the Islamorada case. Upon his election as sheriff, he asked Dalton to transfer to the Key West station. Dalton welcomed the move, since it put him closer to where he lived on Little Torch Key.

Dalton went over his notes with them, and about half-way through, Deputy Daniels came in and dropped off his report. He raised his eyebrows before leaving, as if surprised at Dalton meeting face-to-face with the new sheriff.

When Dalton finished his brief, Diaz said, "This is a high profile case. Riley Gunn has been an aggravation in this community, but he's also a celebrity. News of his murder will flood the airwaves. We need to find his killer yesterday."

"Understood," Dalton said. "We'll get him."

"I know you will, Detective. I'm counting on you."

Back at his desk, Dalton phoned Daniels. "At the crime scene, you said something about Gunn angering people other than those who didn't like his wild parties. What did you mean by that?"

"Well, this is just hearsay, but there could be something to it. Gunn recently filed a lawsuit against Raven Gardner, who owns the Key West Star Hotel and Golf Club. The property is worth over a hundred million, and the suit maintains that she cheated Gunn's grandfather out of his half of the ownership."

"Okay, so what's the hearsay part?"

"Rumor has it that Raven had her lawyers pay Gunn a visit and explain why he should withdraw the suit."

RILEY GUNN'S MOTHER lived on Big Pine Key. Buddy provided Dalton with the address and he headed out to inform her of her son's death. She opened the door wearing a business suit and carrying a purse, as if about to leave for a meeting.

"Ms. Gunn?"

"Yes?"

"I'm Michael Dalton with the Monroe County Sheriff's Office." He displayed his badge.

"Oh, no. What has he done now?" A smile leaked away as she eyed the detectives face.

"Can we go inside?"

"Of course. Come in."

She led him to the living room. When they were seated, he gave her the bad news. Her face contorted as tears streamed down her cheeks. After a minute or so, she pulled a tissue from her bag and mopped the tears. "Was it an overdose?"

"Has he overdosed before?"

"Once before, when he came off a long tour. We got him to the hospital in time."

"I'm sorry. He died from a gunshot wound."

"What? Why would anyone kill Riley? He was so sweet." The waterworks started up again.

Mothers usually thought their sons were sweet. In this case, at least one person didn't agree, either that or someone had a reason to silence him.

"Did your son have any enemies?"

"No, none. His fans and friends loved him."

He gave her a moment, but she didn't say any more. "We need someone to identify the body. Can you do that?"

She blew her nose and sighed. "Yes, I want to see my son."

Dalton called the ME's office and arranged an appointment for her to go in.

"Do you know if he had any life insurance?"

Mopping the last of the tears, she said, "Well, yes, as a matter of fact he did. He took out a policy about a month ago and named his three band members as beneficiaries."

"Do you know the value of the policy?"

"I think it was three million, to be split equally

among them. I don't think anybody expected him to die, though."

Gunn might have known something bad waited for him down the road. Knowledge of the policy by his beneficiaries could also have been the catalyst for his death.

"It's come to our attention that your son recently sued the family that owns a big resort in Key West. Something about them cheating his grandfather out of his share of the property."

She sighed. "I warned him not to do that. Raven Gardner is mean. Do you think she killed him because of it?"

Ignoring the question, he said, "Do you know why he thought he had a chance with them in court?"

"His grandfather had been mounting a lawsuit to be compensated for his part of the property. When he died last year of a heart attack, his lawyers encouraged Riley to go forward with it. They seemed to think he had a good case."

Dalton made notes, said, "Do you know who will inherit his estate?"

"I'm his only living relative. His father died years ago in a car accident."

"So you think everything will go to you?"

"I'm afraid so, but he probably has more debt than assets. These last couple of years haven't been kind to him."

After a pause, he said, "All right. Please let me know if you think of anything that might help explain what happened." He gave her his card.

CROOK MET HIM at the address of the first name on his list of party attendees. Colin Casey played bass for

Redgunn and lived in a cottage on the beach. It was a nice place, but a far cry from Gunn's estate. When Casey opened his door a crack, Dalton said, "Michael Dalton. I called a few minutes ago." He held up his badge for Casey to see.

"Oh, yeah, okay. Hold on." He stepped away, but returned a minute or so later and swung the door open. "Sorry, I was at a party last night," he said, buttoning his shirt. "What's this about?" He spoke with an Irish brogue. Tattoos extended from his wrists into his short shirtsleeves.

Dalton and Crook followed him inside.

The rocker's longish hair looked as if he had stood in a wind tunnel. He had bags under his eyes and piercings in multiple places on his face.

"It's about the party," Dalton said, taking a seat in a cozy living room on a rattan sofa. Other than an empty beer bottle on an end table, the place appeared surprisingly neat.

"Uh-oh. We got a little carried away. Riley likes to crank up the amps. We probably all have hearing loss. Get you a drink? Coffee, or a beer."

Dalton shook his head. "I'm fine, thanks."

"Yeah, me too," Crook said.

Casey stepped over to a kitchenette and got a beer from the refrigerator. He poured half of it into a glass and filled the remainder with tomato juice. "Hair of the dog, you know."

When he returned and got seated, Dalton said, "What time did you leave the party?"

Casey took a slug of the drink. "I think it was about two or two-thirty."

"You brought a guest, right?"

"Sure, Marilyn was with me. Marilyn Coe. She left when I did." Ana Kovich had given him the woman's name.

"Did you or anyone argue with Riley?"

"No, we had a grand time. Why would you ask me that?" He slurped the tomato concoction.

"Riley Gunn died this morning between the hours of 2:00 and 7:00 a.m."

"What?" Frowning, he set his glass down on a side table and leaned forward. "That can't be. I was the last one to leave, and he was fine. You sure it was Riley?"

"Yes, I'm sure. His housekeeper found him."

"Riley, dead. This is too much." Casey put his fingers to his temples and kneaded. He downed the remainder from the glass. When Dalton told him Gunn had been murdered, he just stared, seemingly dumbfounded.

"Are you aware of the insurance policy he took out recently?" Dalton asked.

"Yeah, he told me about it." He glanced at his empty glass.

"It named you and two other band members as beneficiaries for a million each."

Casey's eyes narrowed. "What? You suspect one of us killed him for the insurance money?"

Buddy's phone played an electric guitar version of the Star Spangled Banner. He glanced at the display and said to Dalton, "I need to take this." He stepped outside.

"Sorry, I'm just covering bases," Dalton said to Casey. "Did Ms. Coe spend any time with you after you left the party?"

"Yeah, she stayed here last night. Left right before

your call. And I can tell you, I make a lot more than a million dollars when we're on tour. And my share of record sales is even more than that."

Dalton didn't think Casey did the killing, but they would check with Marilyn Coe for an alibi. "Can you think of anyone who would want Mr. Gunn dead?"

Casey massaged his stomach. "I'm gonna be sick." He jumped up from his chair and headed for the hallway.

Crook came in and said, "That was the security company. They have video of everybody who entered and left Gunn's home last night."

TWO

WHILE WAITING FOR Casey to return, Dalton asked Crook to pull up the website for Redgunn. It indicated that there were three members other than Riley Gunn. Since only two of them were at the party, Dalton compared the list Crook had researched with the names on the site. The drummer, Jimmy Earl, hadn't attended.

Casey returned a few minutes later, his face ashen. He scowled and shook his head. "Riley could be a bitter pill, but I can't imagine anybody wanting to kill him because of it."

"He have arguments with anybody?" Dalton asked.

Shrugging, Casey said, "He and Sheffield got into it a week or so ago."

"The band member?"

"Yeah, lead guitar. He wanted to sing a solo on the album we been working on, but Riley wouldn't go for it."

"Why not?"

Casey gave him a look that said *Why do you think?* "It was Riley's band. He wanted all the glory." It sounded as if Casey might have resented Gunn, too.

"Did they get along okay at the party?"

"Oh, yeah. They'd bumped heads before over the same thing. Sheffield pouted for a few days, but he got over it."

"What about Jimmy Earl? The drummer. Why didn't he come to the party?"

Casey's squinted his eyes, as if trying to remember. "I think Riley said he went to see his ex in Miami."

Dalton made notes in his pad. "Okay, I guess the only other thing I need is the identity of the guests who weren't in the band, other than your dates. Did you know the others? A woman and two men?"

"Riley introduced us when they arrived, but he never said how he knew them. As I remember, the woman's name is Hilda something. Wright, I think. Yeah, Hilda Wright. She sat by herself most of the time, soaking up the booze and staring at her phone. I have no idea why she was there. The two guys were brothers: Stefan and Lars Lange. I remember them best because they hung around with me and Marilyn for a while."

"Do you know if either of the three was in the music business?"

"Yeah, let's see." He closed his eyes and brushed back his tangled mane with his fingers, then said, "The brothers were music producers. They wanted to do a Redgunn album."

DALTON AND CROOK left and drove to the security company on Stock Island. A receptionist in the lobby showed them to a small office where a woman named Rona loaded and ran the videos. She had files for cameras on the front, rear, and each side of the house. The camera at the entrance had no activity until late in the day when the guests began arriving.

"I need an image of each person who enters," Dalton said.

"Electronic or paper?" Rona asked.

"Both."

Rona rolled her eyes, but did as requested. Seven people arrived for the party in four different vehicles: a Range Rover, a Lexus, a Mercedes, and a Cadillac SUV. Dalton recognized Colin Casey, who made his entrance with a date, presumably Marilyn Coe, around 8:30 p.m. in the Rover. Dalton guessed at the identities of the others based on the Redgunn website and what Casey had told him about them. Sheffield and his date arrived in the Caddie about five minutes before 9:00, followed by the Lange brothers in the Lexus a minute later. The blonde woman, presumably Hilda Wright, arrived in the Mercedes about 9:30. She departed first, around midnight. The brothers left around 2:00, along with Sheffield and his date. Casey didn't leave until after 3:00, and his date drove them away. Casey had departed later than he'd said. Maybe just a lapse attributed to booze and whatever else he might have consumed at the gathering.

At 3:50 the video went blank, as if the camera dropped offline.

"What happened there?" Buddy asked.

"Don't know," Rona said. "Looks like somebody deactivated the camera feed."

"How could that happen?"

Rona accessed Gunn's account. "It says here that the owner requested switches for all the cameras so he could turn them off if he wanted to."

So Gunn might have turned off the cameras himself. The only reason he would do that is if he wanted to hide some activity from the video, like a cocaine delivery.

Ana Kovich hadn't appeared in the video, but a silver Toyota had left around 9:10 from the side of the house and headed down the driveway to the street. Dalton asked about the video for that area. When Rona ran through it he spotted Kovich departing from a door next to a three-car garage and getting into the Toyota. There was no other activity after that, and then, as with the entrance video, it went blank around 3:50. They went through to the end of each video but found no other activity after that time.

Dalton said to Rona, "Can you make a DVD of the activity for the entrance and the garage side, beginning a couple of days prior?"

Shrugging, Rona said, "I guess so, it'll take a few minutes."

They waited for the disc and left. In the parking lot, Dalton said he would visit Marilyn Coe. He asked Crook to go by the office and research Hilda Wright and the Lange brothers.

COE LIVED IN a mobile home park on Stock Island. Dalton called her but didn't get an answer. On the chance that she might be home, he went there anyway. A small, tan sedan sat out front. She came to the door bleary-eyed, wearing a filmy gown. A beautiful thirty-something, she had purple hair and a tattoo of a butterfly on her neck. Dalton flashed his badge.

"What do you want?" she asked through the half-open door.

"I need to talk with you about Riley Gunn."

She yawned and then stared for a moment. "Okay,

come in, but make it quick. I need some more sleep before I start my shift at noon."

He entered and sat on the sofa. A wadded fast food bag and a couple of diet soda cans littered a coffee table. Several fashion magazines lay scattered on the floor. She took a seat in a recliner, and the gown rode high as she pulled her legs up beneath her.

"Riley Gunn was murdered sometime this morning," Dalton said.

Her eyes widened. "Oh, wow, he's dead?"

"Yes." As if murder could have any other result.

"Then I guess you already know I was at his place last night for a get-together."

Dalton nodded.

"I liked him, but he could be irritating. He couldn't keep his hands off me every time Colin went for drinks."

Dalton could understand how Gunn might have been attracted. Her looks easily outclassed those of the other women at his house. Even the tattoo was a work of art. She said she had no idea who might want him dead, and her account of what happened after leaving his house compared closely with that of her date.

She picked up a phone from the table next to her chair and glance at the screen. "Did you call me a little while ago?"

"Yes, about twenty minutes ago."

"I left the phone in here so I could get some sleep. You woke me up banging on the door."

"What time did you leave Casey's house this morning?"

"About nine."

"Were you with him the entire time after you left the Gunn residence?"

"Yeah, but I took the sofa, so I didn't get much sleep. I called a taxi this morning and left." She yawned again. "Sorry about Riley. You done?"

"Why'd you sleep on the sofa?"

Another yawn. "Not that it's any of your business, but Colin was too drunk to take me home, and he and I haven't advanced to the bedroom."

"Did you notice anybody at the party using drugs."

"Just Riley. He went down the hall several times during the night. Came back sniffing and rubbing his nose."

"Nobody else?"

"Not that I noticed."

He eyed her for a couple of seconds. "I'm not here to bust anybody on drugs. He had a lot of cocaine on his dresser, and I just want to establish if he had it at that time."

Fixing him with a frown, she said, "You think because I look like a rocker chick I'm into drugs?"

"Sorry, just asking. No disrespect intended."

The frown morphed into a coquettish smile. He felt his face flush.

"That's okay," she said, "just razzing you. The answer is still no, though. You need anything else?"

He shook his head and stood. "That should do it for now. Where do you work, in case I have questions later?" She told him the name of a club on Duval.

Walking him to the door, she said, "You know, you're pretty cute." She gave him another smile that sent his pulse up a few beats. "Call me some time when you're not in cop mode."

As enticing as that sounded, he knew it would be a bad idea…at least while the investigation continued. He thanked her and left. The car was hot when he got in. He started it, cranked the air up high, and drove out of the park. The vision of the scantily clad woman with purple hair remained behind his eyes until the phone chimed. He glanced at the display and answered.

Lola Ann said, "I haven't heard from you in a while." She had a regular news show on Channel Six that had proved beneficial in solving his murder case in Islamorada. An on-air interview with her had helped set a trap for the killer. Their relationship became intimate for a time, but that interest had waned for both of them in the last couple of months.

"Yeah, sorry, still getting acclimated. Burglary and robbery cases have kept me pretty busy."

"Sounds like a waste of your talents."

"Maybe. I don't think my new lieutenant is too sure about my talents. The sheriff brought me in, and I think it miffed him a little."

"Uh-oh, not another micro-manager, I hope."

"We'll see. The jury's still out." He didn't mention the murder case. She would want to run with it, and that probably wouldn't set well with Springer.

"Nothing really exciting going on, huh?"

"No. I'll call if I get anything."

"Sure you will."

He would if she could help him solve his case. "You got it. Maybe we could get together one night and have drinks."

"Yeah, that would be nice," she said. "Kinda busy right now, though. I'll call you."

He smiled as they hung up. They'd had the same conversation about getting together the last three times they had spoken.

Crook called about the mystery guests. "Hilda Wright has a home on White Street near Higgs Beach. I didn't find a local residence for the Lange brothers, so I thought I'd check the hotels. I hit pay-dirt on the third one. They're at the Hyatt, in a suite registered to Lars Lange. We probably should get with them first, since they might leave town."

They met at the hotel. In the lobby, Dalton called the front desk and asked to be connected to the Lange suite.

A man picked up. "Is this Lars Lange?" Dalton asked.

"Yes, who's calling?" He spoke with a slight European accent.

Dalton identified himself and asked if he could speak with him and his brother in person about Riley Gunn's get-together the night before.

Lange hesitated, and then said, "How long will it take you to get here? We have a flight in two hours and haven't completed packing."

"We're downstairs."

"Okay come on up." Lange gave him the room number.

A couple of minutes later, Dalton and Crook entered the suite and sat in easy chairs. The brothers introduced themselves and sat on a sofa facing the detectives. Lars appeared to be around forty, Stefan maybe five years younger.

"Can you tell me your business with Riley Gunn?" Dalton asked.

Lars frowned. "Why is my business with Mr. Gunn of any interest to the police?"

"Because Mr. Gunn was murdered sometime this morning, and we're questioning everyone who attended the gathering at his home."

Stefan gasped. After a pause, he said, "Well, I suppose we made this trip for nothing."

Lars rolled his eyes. "We were wooing Riley for a record deal. It would have been a major coup for us. We're a new label and haven't signed anybody else so famous."

He didn't seem to care about the murder, only what impact it would have on his potential contract.

"Did Gunn say he would sign?" Dalton asked.

"He wanted to give it more thought. It would mean breaking ties with the producers of his previous albums, with whom he had grown dissatisfied."

Dalton asked about the cocaine, and both brothers denied knowing anything about it. They said they had come straight to the hotel after leaving Gunn's house, and had remained there ever since.

"What's your traveling destination?" Dalton asked.

"We're going home to Canada. Our office is located there."

The detectives got the brothers' phone numbers and left. Downstairs hotel security video corroborated the time they had arrived that morning, and didn't show them leaving again.

"WHAT DO YOU THINK?" Dalton asked Crook. They sat at a table in a deli on North Roosevelt.

Crook took a bite of his sandwich and laid it down.

After chewing for a few seconds, he said, "Doesn't sound like we have a suspect yet. Casey and Coe alibi each other. The Lange brothers came here to work a deal, and had everything to lose by Gunn's death."

Nodding, Dalton said, "Maybe we should split up the list. I haven't heard anything on the news yet about the murder, but it'll hit anytime now, and we'll be taking heat on finding the killer. Why don't you take the other band member, Alan Sheffield, and I'll check out the Wright woman and Jimmy Earl, the drummer." It was interesting that Earl had something else to do the night Gunn got murdered.

"Yeah, that'll work. I have to be done by about four-thirty, though. We're starting a gig at a bar tonight, and I need to go in early and set up."

Dalton glanced at the time on his phone. "That gives you a few hours. You should be able to get it done by then."

Crook gave him an expression that indicated he wasn't so sure. "Yeah, if I find Sheffield at home."

Dalton stared for a moment. "Okay, let me know if you can't reach him in time, and I'll get in touch with him myself."

Crook's eyes grew large. "Hey, I don't mean to push off my work. I just have this thing…"

HILDA WRIGHT DIDN'T answer her phone, so Dalton drove by her house. A gate stood out front, and palms, banana trees, and hibiscus obscured the façade and the garage. He drove up to the gate and pressed a speaker button. No response. Same thing when he tried again.

Sitting there at the gate, he punched in the number for Earl, the drummer. A man answered.

"Is this Jimmy Earl?"

"Depends on who's asking."

Dalton identified himself, and Earl said, "You find my car?"

"Sorry, that isn't why I'm calling. You reported a stolen car?"

"Yeah, yesterday. I thought maybe it'd turned up."

"I'll be glad to check on it," Dalton said, "but I need to ask you some questions about Riley Gunn. Is it convenient for me to come to your home?"

"Riley, huh? He in some kind of trouble?"

"You could say that." The worst kind.

Someone in the background said, "Who is it?" A female voice. It sounded sleepy.

"I'm kinda busy right now," Earl said to Dalton. "Can you give me a couple of hours?"

"Sure. 2:00 okay?"

"Yeah, see you then."

A Mercedes pulled up behind Dalton's car and blew the horn. Hilda Wright. He got out, paced back to the driver's side, and held up his badge.

Wright lowered the window. "What is it? I'm in a hurry." She had straight blonde hair, almost to her shoulders, and large blue eyes. An attractive woman.

Dalton told her he needed to talk with her about Riley Gunn. She nodded and activated a remote that opened the gate. He pulled in and parked. She drove by and entered a garage. After a minute or so she came out.

"Can we go inside?" Dalton asked.

She eyed him for a moment. "Let me see your badge again."

When he displayed it, she said, "Michael Dalton, huh?" She gave him the once-over. "I'm a local attorney, and I don't think I've heard of you."

"I'm new in Key West. You can call the office if you want?"

"I'll do that." She took out her phone and selected a number from her address book. A few seconds passed before she told someone her name and asked about Dalton. She nodded her head as she listened and then ended the call. "Okay, you checked out."

They went inside, sat in the living room, and he told her about the murder. "What?" She stared, her face slack, her eyes glistening with tears.

"I'm sorry. He was killed by a gunshot wound to the head."

Droplets slid down her face. She pulled a tissue from her purse and dabbed her eyes.

"How did you know Mr. Gunn?"

She tried a smile. "I was his attorney."

"You and he were close?"

Nodding, she said, "Yes, we were friends. I liked Riley very much." She shook her head. "Why would anybody do such a thing?" She turned away, sobbing.

"We're going to find out. Were you and Mr. Gunn intimate?"

The sobs ended. She peered down at her clasped hands for what seemed like a long time, as if in shock. Dalton waited, and finally she said, "We were for a while, but not in the last month or so."

"Did something happen that caused you to stray apart?"

Shrugging, she said, "The usual story: Riley met another woman. It didn't last long, but I wasn't interested after that."

Jealousy and rejection: two powerful motives for murder.

"So, why did you go to the party?"

"Riley said he wanted to discuss the case with me, but he never did. He just got high and flirted with the other women."

"Are you referring to the lawsuit against the Gardners?"

"Yes. Do you think they had something to do with his death?"

"I can't say at this point. Do you?"

Raising an eyebrow, she said, "That hadn't occurred to me, but Raven seemed pretty angry about it at the deposition."

Dalton nodded. The lawsuit kept coming up. "To your knowledge, did anybody at the party visit Riley's bedroom for cocaine?"

She smirked. "Yes, Riley and the other band members made a parade to his bedroom. I don't think the two women did, though. If fact, they looked a little put out by it."

"You're certain?"

"Oh, yes. Those three were high as a kite."

"Do you know if Riley had a will?"

"Yes, he did. I'll need to get with his mother and other interested parties to go over it. His father is deceased."

"Please let me know when you plan to do that."

She agreed. The others had lied about the drug use. Dalton would need to pay Casey and Coe another visit.

"Okay, that's about all I have, but I need to know about the other woman Mr. Gunn got involved with. Can you tell me her name?"

"Sure, she was at the party. Marilyn Coe."

THREE

DALTON STILL HAD another hour before meeting with Jimmy Earl, so he headed back to Casey's house. When the rocker answered the door, Dalton pushed through. "You lied to me about the drugs at Gunn's house. I have a witness who said you made multiple trips to Gunn's bedroom. I'm not interested in busting you for using, but this is a murder case, and I need to know about his cocaine supply."

Casey's blinking eyes grew large. His hands shook. "Well, I uh—"

"I'm going to arrest you for lying if you don't come clean about this."

"All right. Let's sit down. I don't feel so good." They stepped into the small living room and took a seat. "I did make a couple of trips back there. There wasn't much left the last time I went, though. He said he hadn't been able to link up with his supplier before the party, and he called the guy several times while I was there."

"Who's his supplier?"

"I don't know..."

Dalton shook his head. "I'm warning you; don't lie to me."

"Okay, okay, but I need a drink." He struggled out of his chair, went over to a bar in the corner, and poured a glass of bourbon. Half of it disappeared with the first gulp, the other half with the second. When he returned with a full glass, his hands were steady.

"The guy's name is Wilbur Hess." He took another slug of the whiskey and set it down. His face looked mellow, relaxed, probably the start of an all-day drunk. "I've called on him a couple of times myself. Nothing like Riley, though. He must be Wilbur's best customer."

Too bad they hadn't found Gunn's phone. Dalton needed to prod Buddy about getting with the wireless carrier for the call history.

"How did Gunn know Wilbur?"

"He was one of our roadies for about a year, but selling blow paid a lot more money."

"You have his address and phone number?"

"I don't know where he lives, but I have his phone number." He retrieved it from his contacts and Dalton wrote it down.

"Okay, anything else you omitted or lied about?"

"No, nothing else." The rocker finished his drink and got up for another.

As Dalton got into his car, Jimmy Earl called. "Hey, can we talk tomorrow. My ex just called and said she has an emergency."

"What kind of emergency?"

"She didn't say, but wanted me to come to Miami and help her out."

Dalton didn't like the sound of it, but supposed he could wait. "Okay, what time tomorrow?"

"Maybe ten or after?"

"Okay, I'll see you at 10:00 a.m."

He got Crook on the line. "You have any luck with Sheffield?"

"Yeah, I talked to him and his date," Crook said. "They were both at Sheffield's condo, and they alibi each other. Both of them seemed pretty shocked about the murder. I don't think they had anything to do with it."

"Okay, I spoke with Casey again. He lied about the cocaine, said he used along with Gunn. He also gave up Gunn's supplier, a Wilbur Hess, and said Gunn had been trying to get in touch with him during the party to buy more. I have his phone number, but no address. Maybe you'll have time to research him." He read the number from his pad.

Crook paused on the other end. "You remember, I need to leave by 4:30."

"Yeah, I remember. Do what you can, and if you haven't gotten in touch with Gunn's phone carrier, try to do that, too."

"Aye, aye, Captain," Crook said, an edge in his tone. He hung up.

Good thing Dalton had called when he had, otherwise his partner might have left for the day. He turned on the radio to one of the network news channels. They were talking about the Gunn murder and played a clip from an interview with Sheriff Diaz. He kept it short: "Mr. Gunn was a native son. He grew up in the area and returned to live here last year. We're devoting maximum resources to finding his killer, and while we don't have any solid leads yet, we're interviewing everybody who saw him last. We expect a break in the case soon." *Native son? A little thick, Sheriff.*

On his way to the office, he stopped for two coffees

and a couple of doughnuts. He knew Buddy loved his doughnuts, despite being thin as a rail.

Crook, busy at the keyboard, gave him a smirk when he stepped into his cubicle.

Dalton set the bag and coffee down at his elbow. "Thought you might miss dinner tonight."

Crook stared for a moment and then glanced into the bag and smiled. "Hey, good man." He pulled out a doughnut and began munching before going back to the keyboard.

Dalton went to his desk and brought up the police report for Jimmy Earl's stolen vehicle. He put a flag on the record to notify him when it turned up. A few minutes later, Crook brought a note to Dalton's workstation and laid it down.

"This is the guy." The note bore the drug dealer's name and address. "He must do pretty well. Lives in a waterfront home and drives a new Vette. I found Gunn's wireless carrier, too. They're going to send me a transcript of his calls for the past month."

"Hey, good work." Looking at the time, Dalton said, "You still have an hour before you wanted to leave. How about following me to question Wilbur Hess? He's only a mile or so away, near the airport. You can leave if it takes too long."

"Yeah, that's fine. I talked to Speed. He said he'll set up for the gig, so I don't have to be there 'til 7:00."

"Speed?"

Crook grinned. "Yeah, that's not his real name. We call him that because of all the tickets he's racked up. It's also a pretty cool name for a band member."

Deputy Daniels called. "We spoke with all the neighbors. Nobody heard anything that sounded like a gunshot. They all complained about the music being too loud, but that ended around 2:00 a.m. I'm waiting on some footage from a neighbor's security camera that might give us a glimpse of the victim's driveway entrance."

Dalton thanked him, and he and Crook left in different vehicles. They met at the drug dealer's address, a home that bordered a canal. It sat among many other small houses crammed onto tiny lots. The two detectives parked on the street. A white Corvette sat in the drive, so the owner was probably home. They strode to the entrance, and Dalton pressed the doorbell. No one came, so he tried again a few seconds later. Still no answer.

"Maybe he's asleep," Crook said. "He probably does most of his work at night." He chuckled.

"Yeah, maybe." Dalton gave the door a loud rap, and it squeaked open a crack. "Something's wrong." He drew his weapon, eased the door open about six inches, and called out, "Wilbur Hess? Monroe County Sheriff." No response, but a rattling noise came from somewhere in the house. "Mr. Hess. Are you in there?" The rattling continued. "We're coming in." He pushed the door open and they stepped inside, closing the door behind them. The room had little light, so Crook flipped the wall switch.

The body of a man lay face down on the living room floor. Blood had puddled under his head and spattered the far wall. There was a bullet entry wound slightly above his ear. It appeared similar to the one on Riley Gunn in size and that it had exited the other side of his head. A hole in the center of the blood spatter on the wall indicated the slug might be found there, or somewhere else in the house if it traveled on through. No weapon close by, which would nix suicide. The round had entered the victim's head from the side, as if the killer might have taken him by surprise.

Rattle. The noise came from the corner. Dalton swung his 9mm in that direction, his pulse drumming in his ears. He eased over. A table at the end of the sofa, along with a lamp on top, flipped into the air, and a creature burst out from underneath. It sped by them in a blur, skirting the body, heading for the hallway.

"What was that?" Crook asked, his tone pitched higher than normal.

"Burmese Python." Dalton had been introduced to the species many years before on a black ops mission in an Asian jungle. This snake was about ten feet long and as fat in its middle as the business end of a baseball bat. Probably a young one, since they could grow much larger.

"Oh, man." Crook pressed his palm against his chest, his face ashen. "If it's okay with you, I'm gonna wait in the car."

"Yeah, go ahead. How about calling in the murder?"

"Okay." His partner hurried out the door.

The room felt hot, and Dalton wondered if the air conditioner might be on the blink, or the owner purposely kept the temp elevated to suit the python. He stretched on vinyl gloves and pulled the dead man's wallet from his back pocket. It was fat with hundred-dollar bills. The driver's license displayed a photo of a young man with dark hair, and identified the owner as

Wilbur Hess. He turned the body enough for a positive ID, and then turned it back to its original position and replaced the wallet in the pocket.

It appeared Hess had been standing, or maybe heading toward the small kitchen that adjoined the room. The killer could have been waiting behind the door, or entered at the same time Hess had. After popping him, he had fled, leaving the door ajar in his haste.

The place looked as if it hadn't been cleaned in a long time. Empty beer cans and fast food wrappers littered the sofa and floor. In the kitchen, a huge metal cage sat in the corner, its door wide open. Dalton wondered who had left it that way. A couple of pizza boxes lay open on a dinette table, along with more empty beer bottles. Dirty dishes filled the sink. The refrigerator contained a jar of mayonnaise and a rancid pack of sandwich meat. A drawer in the bottom held clear plastic bags filled with squirrel-sized rats. Pet food.

Easing down the hall, Dalton watched and listened for indications of the snake's presence. It had hidden somewhere, and he didn't want to find it. In the single bedroom, a pile of clothes occupied one corner. The bed was unmade. Its sheets, probably white when new, had turned an uneven shade of beige.

A suitcase sat in one end of the bedroom closet. The top was ajar, held open by articles of folded clothing. The items appeared to have been pulled out in a hurry, maybe during a search. Dalton raked the clothes out of the way, pulled the case into the light, and opened it up. More folded items remained inside, but after closer examination he found a button, disguised as a rivet, that released a false bottom. Bags of white powder, probably cocaine, lay underneath. If the killer had searched for the drugs, he had missed the extra storage in his haste.

Hearing voices, Dalton clicked the bottom into place and slid the suitcase back into the closet. He went to the living room and found two Key West police officers. One knelt over the body, staring at the head wound. Dalton flashed his badge for the other. "The victim's wallet IDs him as Wilbur Hess. I believe he was a drug dealer linked to the murder of Riley Gunn."

The officer just nodded. "You didn't foul the scene, did you?"

"No, I didn't."

"Okay. Key West PD is in charge here. Detectives are on their way. They'll want to talk to you. I'd prefer if you waited outside."

"Sure." Dalton headed out to join Crook in his car.

"The watch commander said this is Key West jurisdiction," Crook said. He seemed to hold his breath, as if thinking Dalton might blame him for bringing in the city police.

"That's fine. Hopefully they'll cooperate."

Crook shook his head. "I wouldn't count on it. We had a dust up with them a couple of months ago on a robbery. One of our deputies mishandled some evidence at the crime scene, and they pitched a fit about it."

Within a few minutes, a car pulled up behind them, and two men exited and headed toward their vehicle. "That's Jack Ringo and Ronnie Culp," Crook said. "Ringo's the tall one. A real jerk. Culp's okay, though."

Dalton got out and walked along with the detectives to the house, briefing them on what had transpired. He explained that the door had been left open, and how the murder related to that of the rock star.

"Yeah, well, we'll see about that," Ringo said. "Wait out here while we go in and take a look. You'll have to go to the station and give your statement."

Dalton nodded. "Yeah, I know."

Ringo gave him a smirk. "Your story better stack up." He turned and headed inside.

Culp followed and said over his shoulder, "He's a lot of talk. Don't take it personal."

When Dalton returned to Crook's car, Crook said, "How'd it go with Ringo?"

"Went just fine."

"You tell him about the snake."

"He'll find out soon enough."

A few minutes later, Ringo rushed out the front door, followed by his partner and the officers. Ringo glared at Dalton, pulled his phone from his pocket, and made a call.

CROOK GAVE HIS statement first and headed out to his music gig. When it came Dalton's turn, Ringo went over his story several times, as if trying to trip him up. His account remained the same, and he didn't leave the Key West Police station until after 6:00.

While in the neighborhood, Dalton found the nightclub where Marilyn Coe worked and went inside. There were plenty of seats at that early hour. He spotted her behind the bar and sat on a barstool nearby.

"Well, if it isn't Mr. Copper," she said, as she approached. "You here on business or do you want a drink?"

"Ginger ale would be good."

"Ah, business."

When she returned with his drink, he said, "Someone told me you had an affair with Riley Gunn. You failed to mention that when we talked earlier."

She shrugged. "That's because I don't know what you're talking about."

"You're saying it's untrue?"

"I've never had a relationship with Riley. I heard he and Hilda Wright had a thing, but you wouldn't know it by the way he avoided her at the party last night. She gave me the evil eye every time he tried to hit on me." Glancing down the bar, she said, "I got customers," and stepped away.

It sounded as if Hilda could have gotten the wrong idea about Gunn's other woman. Assuming Coe was telling the truth. She had lied about Casey not having cocaine at the gathering, so she could be lying about Gunn, too.

She returned a few minutes later. "That the only reason you came to see me?" She gave him that smile, the one that made his heart skip a beat.

He attempted a grin, but felt it probably looked a little silly, especially with his face reddening. "There was something else. Colin Casey admitted to using cocaine last night. You said he didn't."

Her smile evaporated. "That weasel. I thought he probably did, but I didn't want to get him in trouble."

Dalton stared for a few seconds, watching her squirm a little. She added, "He drank so much of Riley's booze, who could tell. He could've done it when I went to the bathroom."

"Do you know Wilbur Hess? Used to be a roadie for the band."

She shook her head. "Must've been before I knew them. You think he killed Riley?"

Ignoring the question, he glanced around the bar. "Looks like business is picking up."

"Yeah, they start pouring in about this time of night. I'll be slammed for a couple of hours before going home."

"Must be good for tips."

"It's okay. I'm not getting rich." She glanced down the bar. "Gotta run for a customer."

When she walked away, he laid a bill on the bar and headed for the door. Turning back, he saw her watching him leave. She fixed him with a mock pout, and he gave her a wave. Something about her...

Before heading home, he stopped at the office and checked his email. CSI Tarver had sent his report of the Gunn murder scene. In the living room and bathrooms, the team had found fingerprints belonging to Gunn, Colin Casey, and Ana Kovich, as well several they couldn't identify. Those of Kovich and Casey were on file from visa applications. The housekeeper's visa had expired two years earlier without a renewal. In Gunn's bedroom, where Dalton guessed the murder had taken place, the CSI team had found the victim's prints and those of Ana Kovich. They'd also found partial prints belonging to Gunn and Casey on the drug paraphernalia.

The prints didn't help much, other than to confirm Casey's admission that he had used the cocaine along with Gunn. The housekeeper had a logical reason for her prints to be found in the victim's bedroom.

Tarver's report indicated that several samples of blood at the scene had been sent to the lab for DNA analysis. They had located the kill slug buried in the wall and identified it as 9mm. Nothing else in the report seemed beneficial in identifying a killer.

Remembering the disc from the security company, he loaded it onto his computer and started it up. It began two days earlier. Few vehicles came and went the entire time. The housekeeper arrived mid-morning each day and left seven or eight hours later. As shown on the video earlier, she remained longer the day of the party. Also that day, a landscape crew came and worked on the lawn and shrubs. They left a little past noon. Another car drove in and out of the garage a number of times over the course of the two days. Dalton checked the motor vehicles database and verified that the car belonged to Riley Gunn. His departures were always in the afternoon, except for one, two days before, when he left at 9:00 a.m. He returned a couple of hours later. Dalton wondered if he might have visited the law office for a meeting about his lawsuit. That reminded him that he needed to talk with Hilda Wright again the next day and get more details about the case. He made a note to visit her, and also the defendant in the suit, Raven Gardner. Finding nothing suspicious about any of the footage, he closed the video.

He wondered if the medical examiner was still in the office. A vehicle had occupied the ME's designated parking spot a few minutes earlier, so he wended his way down the dimly lit hall and found Dr. Bragg at his desk working at a computer.

Bragg turned when he approached the open doorway. "Yes, Detective?"

"I wondered if you'd finished the autopsy of Riley Gunn."

"I have. I'm compiling my findings."

"Anything of significance you can share with me?"

The little man gave him a condescending smile. "No, you'll have to wait for my report."

Dalton's face felt warm. "When do you think you'll get around to sending it?"

"When I'm finished, Detective. I'm not sure how you operated where you came from, but you'll learn that I won't be rushed with my analysis. Now, if there's nothing else…"

Touchy. Muttering unseemly names for the doctor, Dalton went back to this work station and turned off his computer. There wasn't anything else he could do at the present, so he headed toward Little Torch Key. On the way, he stopped at a restaurant on Stock Island and had grilled hogfish, a Key West delicacy.

Dalton lived in a guest cottage at his uncle's marina, where renters of several other cottages and a couple dozen boat slips also called the place home. When he had arrived in the Keys from Chicago, Uncle Eric had invited him to stay until he found a place of his own. Several months had passed since then. The setup was so good he'd had little incentive to move. Eric didn't seem to mind, though, since Dalton compensated him for lost rent and helped with work around the docks.

At that time of the evening, Eric burned tiki torches

on the deck overlooking the marina. Guests often showed up with drinks to relax with friends. As Dalton approached on the winding driveway, his uncle waved. He parked the car and ambled over.

"There's beer in the cooler," Eric said.

Geraldine Beale, a boisterous fifty-year-old and a long-time guest, sat with her husband Charlie. Dalton said hello to them, pulled a bottle from the ice, and took a seat. Cupcake, their fully-grown pet cougar, stepped out from the shadows and nuzzled the side of his face. He scratched the cat's ears and took a long drink from his bottle. Dalton had rescued him from Florida Fish and Wildlife, where he would have been euthanized. His previous owner, who raised him from a cub, had been killed.

Geraldine said, "He's been bumming beer since we got here an hour ago."

As if the cat understood, he went to her chair and rubbed against her arm. *"Rowww."*

"He's so cute." She poured beer into a bowl at her feet and Cupcake lapped it up. "But I think he's had his limit." Shifting gears, her brow furrowed as she said, "I saw the sheriff on TV today, talking about Riley Gunn getting killed."

"Yeah," Dalton said, "I heard about that. Did he say who did it?" Geraldine could be a busybody, and he didn't want her peppering him with questions.

She just stared for a moment, maybe wondering if he knew more. "He said they didn't have any suspects yet." She drank down her beer, said something to her husband that Dalton didn't catch, and stood. "I guess we'll call it a night." She scratched behind Cupcake's ears and she and Charlie stepped off the deck. The cat watched as they made their way down the walkway toward the dock, maybe realizing he'd had his last drink for the night.

"You caught that case, didn't you?" Eric said.

"Yeah, sure did."

"Good. They need to find the killer quick, and you're the one to do it."

Both Eric and Dalton had worked homicides with the Chicago PD. Eric had stayed an entire career. Dalton's career had been cut short. The chief of police had asked him to leave or be fired, fearing his testimony in a corruption case would lead to prosecution for him and other higher-ups in the department. Dalton went back later for a deposition, at the request of state's attorneys, but his testimony had little, if any, effect on the case. It was his belief that dirty cops would hang themselves, and didn't need any help from him.

"It's been a long day," Dalton said. "I'm going to turn in." He headed to his cottage, with Cupcake following. After feeding the cat a pack of ground meat, he brushed his teeth, showered, and got into bed. He lay there only a minute or so before fatigue tugged at his consciousness, and images of a beautiful woman with purple hair crept into his dreams.

His phone chimed, maybe many times, until it brought him up from a deep sleep. Sheriff's Office, 4:18 a.m., appeared on the display. He answered.

"Hey Detective, this is Snyder, the watch commander. Sorry to bother you, but I thought you should know we found the stolen car belonging to a man named

Jimmy Earl. You indicated you wanted to be notified when it turned up."

Dalton took a deep breath and let it out with a sigh. "Okay. So why did you think I'd want to know about that at four in the morning?"

"We found it near Riley Gunn's house. There's blood inside."

FOUR

THE SUN HAD not risen by the time Dalton reached the site where deputies found Jimmy Earl's car. Just around the block from Riley Gunn's estate, the lot was overgrown with palmetto and wild shrubs. He parked behind sheriff's cruisers on the street. A tow-truck driver hooked the car up as he approached a couple of deputies.

"Who found the car?" Dalton asked.

One of them said, "I did. When I drove by, one of the taillights reflected in my headlamps. I saw the blood on the steering wheel when I shined the light inside."

The tow truck driver started the engine and eased Earl's vehicle out of the brush. Dalton hurried over to the cab. "I want to take a quick look inside before you go."

The driver, who looked half asleep, nodded. "Yeah, go ahead."

It was a vintage Camaro with dark green paint. Probably worth a lot of money. He shined his Maglite inside at the wheel and saw the blood. Not much there, but enough. Could be anybody's, including Riley Gunn's. He rounded to the other side and peered through the passenger window. No key in the ignition, and no wires hanging underneath the dash. That made him wonder how the thief, maybe the murderer, had started the engine. Maybe it wasn't stolen at all. Maybe Jimmy Earl parked in the brush, ran over and killed Gunn, and returned to a car that wouldn't start. In that case he would be reluctant to get a tow truck out there so near the murder scene.

Dalton went back to the deputies. "This vehicle might be connected with the Gunn murder. It needs to be impounded."

"Roger that," one of the deputies said. He spoke with the driver and then they got into their cruisers and followed the tow truck out of the neighborhood.

Dalton went to an all-night diner and had breakfast and a couple of cups of coffee. It bothered him that there was no ignition key and no sign of a hotwire. After the CSIs poured over the vehicle, he would need to verify whether or not the ignition had been hotwired. If not, Jimmy Earl would have to explain how someone else got his car key.

He arrived at the office a little after six o'clock and left a note on Lucas Tarver's desk to call him. Tarver phoned a half-hour later. Dalton briefed him on the situation. The CSI lead said they would get right on it.

Lt. Springer walked through the office at seven and stopped by Dalton's desk. "I expected a progress review yesterday evening on the Gunn case."

"We were pretty busy. I can brief you now if you want."

"Yes, please do." He strode away toward his office.

Taking his time, Dalton stopped by the break room for a cup of coffee to carry in with him. When he arrived, Springer gave him a smirk. "I thought you were right behind me."

Ignoring the comment, Dalton took a seat and set

his cup on the edge of the lieutenant's desk. He told
him about their interviews with Gunn's party attendees,
about the drug connection, finding the dealer's dead
body, and the stolen vehicle with blood inside. He took
a sip from his cup and leaned back in the chair.

"I suppose you didn't think finding a dead body was
important enough to report to me."

"We called it in. I thought the watch commander
would pass that on."

Springer waved away the comment, which probably
meant the watch commander did relay the information.
"I got a call on my way in this morning from Detective Ringo of the Key West PD. He said you and your
partner went inside the house and fouled his scene."

"We didn't foul anything."

"He also said you failed to alert him about a dangerous snake in the house."

Dalton furrowed his brow. "There was a snake in
there?"

Springer shook his head. "I don't like getting calls
like that. I expected you to brief me on it rather than
hearing about it from the Key West PD."

Routine reporting to the LT sounded like a good duty
for Buddy. Dalton stood. "Sorry, I have a meeting." He
picked up his coffee cup and left. Back at his desk, he
thought about the discussion with the lieutenant. The
guy had been too preoccupied with the lack of an update and the call from Ringo to realize the significance
of finding Jimmy Earl's vehicle.

Time to talk to Earl. Dalton passed by Crook's
desk on the way out and told him where he was going.
"While I'm gone, how about checking around with

taxis and hired cars that Jimmy Earl or someone else might've called for a ride after ditching the Camaro in the woods."

Crook nodded. "Okay, I can do that." He looked hung over, his eyes a network of crimson.

Jimmy Earl lived in an aging, waterfront house in Marathon. A late model sports car sat in the driveway. Dalton parked behind it, went to the door, and knocked. Earl peeked out a minute or so later, his hair disheveled, eyes puffy. The detective flashed his badge.

"It's only eight o'clock," Earl said. "I thought you were coming at ten."

"That was before we found your vehicle."

"You didn't need to come so early to tell me that."

"Yes, I did. Let's go inside."

Shrugging, Earl stepped out of the way and waved for him to enter. The room looked tired, like the house: furniture past its prime, dingy drapes, cheap reproductions on the wall.

"Have a seat on the sofa. I'll be right back." He went around a breakfast counter into the kitchen. "You want coffee?"

"No, thanks."

He returned a couple of minutes later carrying a cup and took a seat. "I heard about Riley. He must've gotten into something really bad."

Like Casey, ink swirled up both of Earl's arms. Dalton supposed that was the case with most musicians. "We found your car around the corner from his house. It had blood on the steering wheel."

"Huh." A moment later his eyes widened. "You think whoever stole the car could've killed him?"

"Maybe. The blood analysis might confirm it. When did you realize the car was gone?"

"Day before yesterday. I hadn't driven the Camaro in a few days. Thought I'd take it into town. When I went to the garage it was missing."

"You have the keys for it?"

"Yeah. Why do you ask that?"

"Can I see them?"

The drummer got up and stepped down the hall. He came back and showed Dalton a set of keys.

"Do you have a spare set?"

Earl raised an eyebrow. "This *is* the spare set. I couldn't find the ones I usually have hanging in the kitchen."

Dalton took out an evidence bag and asked him to drop the keys inside. "I need to take them for analysis."

"Why all the questions about the keys?"

"Because whoever took your car had the ignition key. Who's been in your kitchen?"

"I have a housekeeper who comes a couple of times a week." Earl scratched his head and took a sip of coffee. "Some girlfriends have been over. That's all I can think of."

"Any of them in the kitchen when you weren't?"

"Just the housekeeper, but I don't think she would've taken the keys. She's a little Cuban lady who has grandchildren."

Dalton just nodded and stared for a moment. "Tell me where you were night before last."

"You think it's me? You think I killed Riley?" The volume of his voice rose, his tone pitched higher.

"Just tell me."

"I was with my ex-wife in Miami." He shook his head and sipped his coffee.

"What time did you get there and leave?"

Earl shrugged, took his time answering, as if pouting. "Got there around 7:00 p.m. and left the next morning about six."

"Will she corroborate that?"

"Yeah, of course."

"Okay, I'll need to speak with her." Dalton got her name, address and phone number. "Any bad blood between you and Riley?"

"No more than normal. We got along like cats and dogs. It was always his way or the highway."

Glancing at the threadbare furniture, Dalton said, "You own this place?"

"No, it's rented."

"Did you know about the insurance policy Gunn took out for the band members?"

The drummer smirked. "Sure. He went out of his way to let us know how well he was taking care of us in case something happened to him."

"You gamble, have expensive habits?"

"That's none of your business." He stood. "Maybe it's time you left."

"Sit down. I'm not going anywhere. I'm guessing you need your part of the insurance proceeds."

Earl didn't reply, but sighed and dropped back into his chair.

"I'll take that as a 'yes.'" Dalton made notes in his

pad, and then said, "In case you haven't heard, Riley's cocaine connection, Wilbur Hess, got murdered yesterday." He watched Earl's face for any sign that he knew.

"Huh, that's too bad," Earl said, his expression not giving away anything.

"Were you a customer?"

Earl eyed him for a couple of beats, maybe deciding whether or not to lie.

"I'm not interested in busting you for using."

"Yeah, well, I had a bit of a problem, mainly because of Wilbur. That's why Coleen left me."

Dalton told him he had enough information for the time being. "Don't go anywhere. We might need to talk again later."

Earl gave him a smirk and ushered him out the door.

In the car, Dalton sat there and called CSI Tarver. "Did you find any prints on the steering wheel?"

"We found prints that match the owner, Jimmy Earl, which could've been there before the vehicle was stolen. We didn't find any prints in the blood." That meant the murderer wore gloves. Earl's prints being on file indicated he had been charged with something in the past. He made a note to ask Buddy to research that.

"You send off the blood for analysis?"

"Yes, a courier took it. It should be at the lab in an hour or so."

"Can you get them to put a priority on it?"

"I can ask, but they're always busy."

"Do your best. I'd bet a paycheck that it's Riley Gunn's blood."

He hung up, phoned Earl's ex-wife, and asked about his alibi.

"Yeah," she said, "he was here that night. Left early yesterday morning."

"Was he in your presence the entire time?"

"Uh, well, no. We didn't sleep together, if that's what you're asking. He slept in the guest room and left before I got up at nine."

"So he could've left earlier than 6:00 a.m.?"

She hesitated, maybe wondering if she was about to get her ex in trouble, and then sighed. "I guess so. I was out like a light after midnight. You think he killed Riley?"

Ignoring the question, he said, "Do you know about his money troubles?"

"Oh, yeah. That's the reason he was here, asking me for cash. I got everything in the settlement."

"Did you give it to him?"

"No. The last two times I did that he squandered it on drugs and gambling at the tracks." If she didn't see him after midnight, that gave him plenty of time to get back to the Keys and murder Gunn. He probably figured a million dollars in insurance proceeds would solve his problems.

Dalton drove to the impound lot with the key he had gotten from Earl. The car sat in the sun. He stretched on gloves and opened the door. After waiting a minute or so for heat to escape, he got inside. The starter just gave a weak *click*. He popped the hood release, got out to take a look underneath, and found a loose battery cable. It seemed *too* loose to have gotten that way without help. Upon touching the cable bolt, it fell into his hand, so he screwed it back into place and tried the starter again. The V-8 engine came to life with a throaty rumble.

The original theory of how Earl might have parked, killed Gunn, and returned to a car that wouldn't start, had seemed plausible. But the loosened battery cable was problematic. And there were other questions that begged an answer. How did Earl get into the house without being discovered. Did he know the cameras would be turned off, or did he just get lucky? And he didn't have a vehicle to follow Wilbur Hess home and kill him. Did he do that later? Or did he interrupt the drug deal, kill Gunn, and force Hess to drive him to Hess's house. If so, how did he get home from there, several miles away?

When he got back in his car, he turned on the air full blast and phoned Key West PD. He asked for Ronnie Culp, thinking he might be more cooperative than Ringo. The detective picked up.

"This is Michael Dalton with the sheriff's office. I met you when you came out for the Wilbur Hess murder."

"Yeah, I remember."

"Well, as I mentioned before, I think whoever killed Riley Gunn also killed Hess. I'm trying to put together a sequence and wondered if you have a time of death yet for your case."

After a short hesitation, Culp said, "No, we don't have that yet. Jack went over and talked to the ME. He said they're backed up, and a drug dealer is probably low on their list."

"Okay, I'll check back."

"Yeah, do that. Jack doesn't think the case is related to yours, but if we find out otherwise we'll let you know." They hung up.

Dalton sat there, the air cooling his face, and thought about the evidence against Jimmy Earl. It seemed a little too convenient that his car was found with blood on the wheel. The drummer had his personal problems, but he didn't seem stupid. If he had blood on his hands after killing Gunn, he would have shed the gloves before getting inside, or cleaned it up afterward. And there was the question of the battery cable, which appeared to have been loosened on purpose. There were too many holes that seemed to point to a frame. Earl was an easy target. He needed the insurance money, and he blamed Wilbur Hess for his addiction. But who else would have a reason to kill Gunn and Hess? He thought about the lawsuit and called Hilda Wright. They agreed to meet at her office an hour later.

Since he had an hour to kill, he swung by the office. Crook stared at his computer screen, his fingers idle on the keyboard.

"I forgot to ask earlier," Dalton said. "How'd your jam session go?"

Crook made a slow turn to look his way. "The crowd kept us there until midnight, and the manager sent plenty of beer during the breaks. I don't see how we played the last hour, but the patrons were probably drunker than we were. We got taxis home, and I had to go back for my car this morning."

Dalton brought him up to date on the stolen car and his conversation with Earl.

"You think he did it?" Crook said.

"I'm keeping the options open."

Crook pulled a bottle of aspirin from his desk drawer and swallowed a couple with a sip of coffee. "Oh, yeah, I talked with the taxi companies and the hired cars that are available around here. None of them picked up anybody near Riley Gunn's place that night. Whoever ditched that Camaro must've had a friend pick him up."

"Huh, that's too bad. I was hoping we'd have a driver who could identify the guy. I'm meeting Hilda Wright in a few minutes to talk about Gunn's lawsuit."

"You want me to come along?" Crook asked, his tone listless, as if not interested in leaving his desk.

"I'd rather you stay here and get more research on the band. See if we can find out anybody else who might have a score to settle with Gunn. Look up Jimmy Earl's arrest record, too. He popped up when Tarver ran prints from his car."

Crook gave a mock salute. "I'm on it, Brother."

HILDA WRIGHT'S FIRM occupied the second floor of a re-stored, two-story conch house a few blocks off White-head Street. A stair along the side led up to the entrance. Dalton climbed the steps and went in the door to a cool lobby. No one appeared to be minding the store.

A young man in a yellow, casual shirt came up the hall and stopped. "Can I help you?"

"Michael Dalton to see Hilda Wright." Dalton flashed his badge. "I'm a few minutes early."

Yellow Shirt furrowed his brow. "What's this about?"

"You can ask Hilda when you go get her."

The young man gave him a smirk and made a pop-ping sound with his tongue as he walked away.

A minute later, Hilda came into the room with several folders in her arms. She gave him a smile, which he hadn't seen during his previous talk with her. "I have papers strewn about in my office. Let's go down the hall."

They entered a conference room overlooking a park at the rear of the building and sat at the end of a long table. "I apologize for our new law clerk. He said you were rude to him, but I'm sure he started it."

Dalton shook his head. "He was just a little nosy, or maybe protective over you."

Her face reddened as she laid the folders on the table. "All right. What is it you want to know about the law suit?"

"Mr. Gunn's mother gave me some background on how your firm encouraged Riley to pick up the suit when his grandfather passed away. Can you tell me the amount you were claiming?"

"Certainly. That's part of the public record. The grandfather, Mr. Barry Gunn, initiated the action about a year before he died. At the time, we estimated the value of the Key West Star Resort at $140 million. We sued for half the value as Mr. Gunn's lawful share in the property."

"What's the basis for his claim?"

"Mr. Gunn and Carlton Gardner purchased the land where the resort now resides about a dozen years ago. They never developed anything on it because both men went broke when the real estate market tanked. The land sat idle for a long time after that. Then, after Mr. Gardner died a few years ago, Raven, his grand-daughter, showed Mr. Gunn an environmental report that indicated the property had served as a dumping ground for hazardous waste. She offered to buy out his share for $100,000. Mr. Gunn was ill at the time and desperately needed the money, so he accepted. Then, two years ago an environmental engineer came to him and said a man had attempted to hire him to write a phony contamination report without ever looking at the site. He said he didn't believe there was ever any hazardous waste, and he agreed to testify to the encounter. Mr. Gunn filed suit, but died a few months later. Riley picked up the case, but now he's dead, too." Moisture glistened in her eyes.

"Do you know if Mr. Gunn's mother will proceed with the case?"

Hilda wiped a tear with her fingers. "She said she'll think about it."

Dalton wondered if Raven Gardner was worried enough to kill Riley Gunn to stop the court action.

"I heard Gardner's lawyers paid Riley a visit. Were you there for the meeting?"

"No, I was not. He said they showed up unannounced and told him they would ruin his music career if he didn't drop the suit. It shook him up."

"I need their names and phone numbers. I'd also like the name of the environmental engineer you mentioned."

She gave him the information and he stood, as if to leave. "Oh, yeah, I wanted to mention that I spoke with Marilyn Coe about Riley. She said she's never had a relationship with him."

Her brow furrowed. "Well, he fawned all over her at the party."

"So you just assumed she was the other woman?"

"Yes. He never told me a name, just that he had somebody else."

"Do you have any idea who it might've been?" With others having alibis, and the girlfriend's name seemingly a secret, she could be important to the investigation as a suspect or a witness.

"No, I don't." She snapped the words, grabbed up her folders, and headed out the door.

Back in the car, he phoned Crook. "I just left Hilda Wright's office. She said Raven Gardner's law firm threatened to ruin Riley Gunn's music career if he didn't drop the lawsuit against their client. Have you found any dirt on him that might've caused them to think they could do that?"

"Not so far, just partying binges in the far corners of the world. That's to be expected with rock stars, though. It doesn't seem to hurt their popularity any."

"Okay, keep at it. There has to be something out there that they thought they could hold over his head."

"I did look up Jimmy Earl's record. He was arrested a few years ago in Jacksonville, charged with domestic battery against his wife. The charges were dropped later when his wife admitted she was actually the one doing the battering. There's also a couple of DUIs that landed him in jail for a few days each. That's all I found, though."

ACCORDING TO HILDA WRIGHT, the Law Office of Douglas Vici represented Raven Gardner. Dalton phoned and made an appointment for 1:00 p.m. His stomach reminded him that he hadn't eaten since 5:00 a.m., so he stopped at a food truck and got a sandwich. Still having a few minutes to kill, he located the office and parked on the street about fifty yards away in the shade of a Royal Poinciana. He left the car running, air on full blast, while he ate and read over his notes. On the first interview with Hilda, he had written Marilyn Coe's name, so he struck through it and wrote *mystery woman—need to find*. He made a note by the environmental engineer's name, Blake Owen, to check him out, in case he could identify the person who asked him for the phony report.

As he looked up from his pad, he saw a limo turn into Vici's driveway and drive to the rear of the building, out of sight. He pulled into traffic and turned in at the law office. Rather than park, he eased the car around the building until he could see the rear of the limo and wrote down the plate number. After backing up and parking in the lot to the side of the building, he phoned Crook again.

"Hey Buddy, I want you to run a plate for a limo."

"Okay, shoot."

He gave him the number, and Crook said, "Okay, I'll call you right back with it. I found something on Riley Gunn. Not sure if it's significant or not, but it's the only thing I've come up with so far. About eighteen months ago, while touring in Thailand, he spent a day in the hospital. The story said he claimed to suffer some kind of stomach ailment, but the author suspected he'd overdosed. After that, he canceled the rest of the Asian tour."

"Huh, keep digging and see if you can learn more about it. I'm about to go into a meeting, so I'll call you after that on the plate number."

"Okay, later." They hung up.

Inside, Vici greeted him at the door and led him to a conference room. Dalton noticed a mirror at one end, beyond a long table. Guessing it was one-way glass, he thought they probably had a video camera behind it to record their meetings. He also wondered if someone might be sitting back there watching.

"So, Detective Dalton, what can I do for you today?" Vici was a small, swarthy man with thick glasses. He took the specs off and laid them on the table. His eyes seem to shrink by half.

"As I mentioned on the phone, I'm investigating the murder of Riley Gunn, and I understand he had a lawsuit against your client, Raven Gardner."

Vici just nodded.

Dalton continued. "Apparently, Mr. Gunn told more than one person that you visited his residence and threatened to ruin his music career if he didn't drop the suit."

Returning the glasses to his face, Vici said, "If Mr. Gunn said that, he was lying. I did visit his house, but I never threatened him. I told him his grandfather was not of sound mind to file such an irrational claim, and hoped he would be more sensible. He declined, of course, and I left. Simple as that. No threat whatsoever."

"All right. I assumed that would be your answer, but I wanted to hear you say it. You know it's a felony to lie to a police officer."

Vici bristled. "I'm well aware of the law, Mr. Dalton. Now, if there's nothing else, I have other appointments."

Dalton gave him a smile and walked out without saying anything further. He started the car and pulled out of the lot into traffic. A moment later he noticed the limo entering the street and accelerating, as if to catch up. It reached his car and started around, the large engine roaring. When even with him, rather that continuing, the limo edged over, forcing him to the edge of the street. It continued toward his car until he rode up on the curb and had to slam on brakes to keep from hitting a tree. The limo sped ahead. Its windows were nearly black with tint, so he hadn't seen anybody inside.

Dalton sat there, waiting for his heart rate to normalize, and called Crook. "Hey, Buddy, you find that license number yet?"

"Yeah, the vehicle belongs to a corporation registered in China."

FIVE

ACCORDING TO CROOK, the limo belonged to Eon Harbor International, incorporated in Hong Kong in 1988. The company owned property in Asia, Europe, and the Americas. Dalton wondered if it had a stake in the Key West Star Resort, and if it had something to do with the threat Vici made to Riley Gunn. He drove to the resort, which sat on a couple of acres fronting Key West Bight. Inside, he found the executive offices and asked to see Raven Gardner. The receptionist, a pretty brunette, said he would need an appointment. He showed her his badge. "I'm with the Monroe County Sheriff's Office, and I need to talk with her about the murder of Riley Gunn."

She leaned forward and squinted to read the badge, then gave him an uncertain look. "Have a seat and I'll tell her you're here."

He waited almost thirty minutes before going into the executive's office. Raven Gardner had long, dark hair, blue eyes, and a warm and beautiful smile. Standing nearly as tall as Dalton, she gave him a firm handshake. "Detective Dalton, sorry for the wait. It's been a madhouse today." She offered coffee or water and he declined.

"As I mentioned to your receptionist, I'm investigating the Riley Gunn murder."

"Yes, such a sad thing. I liked Riley a lot. What can I do to help?"

"It concerns the lawsuit he filed against you. I've been told that your law firm threatened him if he didn't cease and desist."

Her eyes widened. "What? That's news to me. Who told you that?"

"A person close to the victim."

"Was this person present when this alleged threat occurred?"

"No, Mr. Gunn communicated it immediately after it happened."

She remained silent for a couple of beats and then said, "Well, I don't know what to say. I certainly never asked anyone to intervene. Even with the court action, Riley and I remained on speaking terms. We were actually very close at one time; he and I dated when we were in high school."

"According to his attorney, he wanted half your fortune."

Smiling, she said, "He knew the lawsuit was frivolous, and I wasn't worried about it. I think he just wanted me back, but I moved on after our teen years."

"What about the claim that you purchased his grandfather's land under false pretenses?"

She waved the comment away. "That land was contaminated. I gave Mr. Gunn a fair price, and I can prove I paid to clean it up."

Dalton wondered who was lying, whether the land was contaminated or not. "Are you familiar with Eon Harbor International?"

Her face seemed to flush, and she hesitated before saying, "Yes, I am. They invested in my resort."

"How much did they invest?"

She frowned. "I don't see how that has anything to do with Riley's murder. Now, if you don't mind, I'm late for an appointment."

"Has your law firm represented you for a long time?"

Standing up behind the desk, she said, "I'm sorry, but you need to leave."

So he had hit a nerve. He thanked her and headed to the door, but turned around. "I'll probably need to speak with you again."

In the car he phoned Blake Owen, the environmental engineer. After identifying himself, he said, "Hilda Wright gave me your name. She said you were going to testify on Mr. Gunn's behalf about the absence of contamination in the land his grandfather owned."

Owen hesitated for a couple of seconds before saying, "Mr. Gunn was murdered. I assumed there wouldn't be a lawsuit anymore."

"Hilda Wright said Riley's mother might pick it up."

"Well, I've reconsidered."

"You're not going to do it?"

"Uh, no, I'm not. I'm an old man, and I don't remember things so well anymore."

It seemed that Riley's murder had caused his memory to lapse.

"Do you know the name of the firm that developed the contamination report?"

"Sorry, but I don't want to get involved any further." He hung up.

Dalton drove to his office and checked email. The

ME had sent a message. He estimated the time of death between 4:00 and 5:00 a.m., which was soon after the time Gunn's security cameras had shut down. As expected, Dr. Bragg said Gunn had died from the gunshot to the head. From the blood spatter on the wall, it appeared he had been standing when shot. The angle of the wound indicated that the shooter had probably been a few inches taller than Gunn's six feet.

CSI Tarver had already confirmed the caliber of the slug they'd dug from the wall as 9mm. It would make a lot of noise. Deputy Daniels had said none of the neighbors heard a gunshot, but they had heard the music. That probably meant the shooter had used a noise suppressor, which hinted at a professional hit.

Remembering the conversation with Daniels, Dalton picked up the phone and called the deputy.

"You mentioned yesterday the possibility of some video from a neighbor's security camera."

"Yeah, it just came in a couple of hours ago. I have to warn you, though, the camera is aimed at the neighbor's driveway. Gunn's is a long way off, across the street. It shows some vehicles entering and leaving Gunn's place, but the images are pretty poor. I'll put it on the network and send you a link." They hung up.

A few minutes later Dalton saw the email pop up. He opened it, followed the link to the video, and fast forwarded to 3:50 a.m., the time when Gunn's camera had shut down. About ten minutes later a white vehicle entered Gunn's driveway. Even though the image was grainy, the car looked like the white corvette belonging to Wilbur Hess. Ten seconds later, an SUV entered. The plate numbers were not visible on either.

The visitors remained there for about twenty minutes before the car came out and the SUV followed. Nothing else happened until a few minutes before 8:00 when a different car entered. He assumed it was the housekeeper.

The two vehicles arriving about the same time meant the drivers probably knew each other, and both knew Gunn's cameras would be offline. Dalton wondered if lawyer Vici, or someone from Eon Harbor, knew Hess. He also wondered how much of the Key West Star the Chinese company owned.

Crook came by and took a seat. "Tell me what happened."

"Hilda said Douglas Vici, a lawyer, is the guy who threatened Gunn, so I went to see him. The limo drove into his driveway right before I did and tried to hide in back. When I went inside and confronted Vici about the threat, he denied it. I sensed that somebody was watching from an adjacent room, and as soon as I left, the limo pulled out and ran me off the road. When you told me who owned it, I wondered if they had a stake in Raven Gardner's resort, so I decided to go see her. She wasn't very cooperative, but she did confirm that Eon Harbor is part owner. You know how to find out the amount they invested?"

"I'll give it a try. If I can't, I have a friend who probably can." He got up and started toward his workstation.

"Oh, Buddy?"

Crook turned around. "Yeah?"

"How do you like briefing the LT?"

His partner gave him a cagey smile. "Not on my list of fun things. Why?"

"He wants daily updates."

The smile leaked away and he sighed. "Okay, I'll do it, but it'll cost you."

"Yeah, what's the price?"

"Fresh doughnuts every morning." He stepped away.

A few minutes later, Crook called. "Eon owns eighty percent of the Star Resort."

"Huh, how'd you find that out?"

"I know somebody in the state office in Tallahassee."

"You have an address?"

"Yeah."

Dalton wrote it down. It was the same as the Key West Star Resort. "Okay, thanks. I'm headed out. Don't forget to brief Springer." Crook hung up on him.

A MAP INSIDE the resort lobby didn't indicate any offices on the premises. Dalton asked a young man at the counter about Eon Harbor.

"That doesn't ring a bell. Let me look it up." He tapped some keys on his computer, and a few seconds later said, "I'm not showing anything for that name. Are you sure you have the correct address?"

"Pretty sure."

The man shrugged. "I can check with our executive office. They should know." He punched a button on the phone and talked with someone. When he hung up he said, "They didn't seem to know anything about that company."

"Okay, maybe I did get the wrong address. Thanks."

He went to his car and drove around the building to a location for employee parking. A gate with a card reader prevented him from entering, but he had a view of the entire lot, and didn't see a limousine. When he returned to the customer lot, he found a space that enabled him to watch for vehicles entering and leaving the employee area.

Fifteen minutes later a limo eased down the driveway toward the gate. It had the same license plate as the one that had run him to the curb. Dalton got out of the car and hurried to the lobby. Within a couple of minutes, an Asian man wearing a suit and tie entered from a door marked Employees Only and headed to the elevators. He got on, the door closed, and the lighted indicator at the top stopped on 4. Dalton got into a second car, ascended to the same floor, and exited as the limo driver used a card key on a lock down the hall. After he entered, Dalton approached and knocked. The driver opened the door and gave him a blank look. Up close he looked fit, small in stature, and no more than mid-twenties.

Dalton flashed his badge. "I need to see whoever is in charge here."

Without saying anything, the man closed the door. After a few seconds he came back, let him in, and motioned for him to follow. He led him down a hallway to a large corner office with a panoramic view of Key West Bight. Another Asian man stepped out from behind a mahogany desk. He also wore a suit and tie. It looked expensive, like the office.

"I am William Chan. And you are?" He spoke with no accent, his diction perfect.

Dalton introduced himself and held up his badge.

Chan scrutinized the credential, then nodded and gestured toward a chair. "Please sit." After taking a seat behind the desk, he said, "What is it that you want, Detective Dalton?"

"Your driver ran me off the road earlier today."

"I think you must be mistaken. My driver has been here all day."

"It was the same limo that just returned to the hotel lot."

Chan smiled, caught in a lie. "Then it must have been an accident."

"I don't think so. He deliberately edged me over."

Nodding, Chan said, "Then I ask you again, what do you want?"

"I'm investigating the murder of Riley Gunn, the musician. I know you're affiliated with Douglas Vici's law firm because I saw your limo at his place of business right before it attempted to run me over."

Chan didn't say anything, so Dalton continued. "Gunn told his attorney that Vici threatened him if he didn't drop his lawsuit against Raven Gardner."

Shrugging, Chan said, "If that is true, what would it have to do with me?"

"You own this property, and Ms. Gardner is only a figurehead. I think Vici was working on your behalf in threatening Gunn."

"That is absurd." Chan scowled. "We do not threaten anyone."

"What kind of dirt did you have on Gunn?"

"The more you talk, the less sense you make." He stood and said to the driver, who had remained in the corner of the room, "Please show the detective out."

On his way to the door, Dalton turned and said, "Some deputies will come around to talk about the incident with the limo. They'll probably impound it and arrest your driver."

Chan just stared, the scowl still in place.

In the car, Dalton started the engine, adjusted the air conditioner as cold as it would go, and sat there for a few minutes. Although not his intention, he thought if anybody from Eon was watching, maybe it would make them nervous. He wondered if the threat to Gunn was related to the Thailand story Buddy had mentioned, and decided to call Jimmy Earl.

"You check my alibi?" Earl asked.

"Yeah. Your ex said she went to bed at midnight, and you were gone when she got up at nine the next morning. It didn't instill confidence in your story. But that's not the reason I'm calling. Do you know what happened on your Asian tour with Redgunn that landed Riley in a Thailand hospital?"

Earl hesitated before answering. "He said he thought it was food poisoning."

"I read an article from around that time that said he probably overdosed."

Another hesitation. "Well, I guess it doesn't matter now. When I went to get him at the hospital he told me he remembered going to his room with a woman. They shared some drugs and he passed out. When he woke up, he was on the floor. Some men were there, slapping his face, asking what he did with the woman. There was blood all over his clothes and on the bed. He didn't remember what'd happened before losing consciousness, but assumed it was bad and thought they were going to kill him for it. Then one of them grabbed him and he felt a prick to his neck. The next thing he knew, he woke up in the hospital. It scared him so bad he canceled the rest of the tour and we headed home."

Eon could have set up the scene to scare him, but why would they do that? At that point, the grandfather was probably still alive, and Riley wouldn't have had anything to do with the suit. Dalton thanked him and they hung up. He wondered when the old man had died and searched obits using his phone. Upon finding the one he wanted, he called Crook.

"Hey, Buddy, what was the timeframe of Riley Gunn's hospitalization in Thailand?"

"Hold on." A minute later he said, "The story was published on the tenth of November, year before last, and it mentioned that Gunn had just left the hospital."

"Jimmy Earl told me what happened. It looks like somebody, maybe Eon, set Gunn up to think he had hurt or killed a woman he was with. Then they drugged him and dropped him off at the hospital."

"Nasty business," Crook said. "Maybe they did it for leverage in the lawsuit his grandfather had against the resort."

"It's curious that the grandfather died about that time."

"You think they killed him?"

"It crossed my mind. We need to find out if an autopsy was done."

"Okay, I'll check on it. By the way, I got the call history from Riley Gunn's phone. The carrier sent it this morning. He called the same number a bunch of times that evening, up to 3:00 a.m. I checked, and it was Wilbur Hess's phone. Then Hess called back at 3:45, and stayed on the line about three minutes."

"That's right before Gunn shut off the cameras. Any other calls?"

"Not after that. There were several other numbers Gunn interacted with, but I couldn't find owners. Must've been burners." Dalton asked him for the numbers, along with Gunn's, and wrote them down.

"Huh, that's interesting. Wonder what he was up to."

"Sounds like he was doing something somebody wanted to hide. Maybe groupies that wanted to remain anonymous."

"Okay, thanks, Buddy." They hung up.

The calls supported the theory that Gunn and Hess had connected and Hess visited him right after the call. But who drove the second vehicle in the neighbor's security video? Maybe someone from Eon?

Vici could have threatened the old man with the Thailand incident involving his grandson. A threat like that could have caused his heart to fail. Or he might have told them where to go, and they killed him in a way that resembled heart failure. They could have tried the same threat with Riley after he picked up the lawsuit. Maybe it didn't work then, either, so they killed him for it. A lot of ifs, but Dalton didn't consider it a big stretch. A lawsuit worth $75 million in a fraudulent land deal was a powerful motive, and the people of Eon Harbor had the means to carry out such an elaborate scheme.

Crook called back a few minutes later as Dalton headed to the office. "No autopsy on Barry Gunn. The coroner's report said his death was due to natural causes. He was 81 years old and in poor health."

"Too bad they didn't autopsy," Dalton said.

"Uh-oh, Springer just passed by my cubicle and looked in. Wonder what he wants."

"Probably ready for his afternoon update."

Crook hung up on him.

Dalton pulled into a parking spot at the office a few minutes later and got out. Jack Ringo stood there next to a car, as if waiting, and headed over to him. "You have a minute?" Ringo asked.

"Sure, what's up?"

"The mayor got a call from a guy named William Chan. He said you've been harassing him." Ringo stared, as if measuring Dalton's response.

"I questioned him about a threat made to Riley Gunn not long before his murder."

"You think Chan threatened him?"

"Actually, his lawyer Douglas Vici did. Right after I questioned him, Chan's limo driver ran me off the road."

"Sounds like you had a good reason to lean on him. I don't like getting pressure from politicians concerning their cronies. Chan probably contributed to the mayor's campaign. If anybody asks, tell them I chastised you about it." The detective grinned.

"How's the Hess investigation going?"

The grin faded away. "You might be right about the two murders being connected. We need to get together and compare notes."

"Anytime, the sooner the better."

"I left my notes at the station. Can you drop by there later?"

Dalton agreed and went inside where he caught a glimpse of Crook sitting in Springer's office. He went to his desk and printed off the crime scene and autopsy emails. Thirty minutes later he sat in a conference room at the Key West Police Department.

Ringo asked him to go first. He went over the potential suspects that had provided alibis, the fact that Gunn's security cameras went off a few minutes before his murder, the neighbor's video showing two vehicles coming and going, and the interviews with Hilda Wright, Douglas Vici, and William Chan about the threat against Gunn. He also told him about Earl's stolen car with blood on the wheel.

"Sounds like he's your guy. You said his alibi didn't hold up."

Shaking his head, Dalton said, "I think the blood in the car was an attempted frame. The neighbor's video was pretty grainy, but I'm pretty sure whoever killed Gunn drove in behind Hess. If Earl had done it, he would've either walked in, or drove his Camaro in. I didn't see either on the video."

"What if he went in the back door, or through the garage?"

Dalton shrugged. "I suppose he could have, if he had a key, but finding the car with blood on the wheel was a little too perfect. And somebody had disabled the battery cable."

Ringo stared, as if thinking, and then shook his head. "Okay, then, why do you think this threat by the lawyer is so important?"

"It goes back to something that happened to Riley Gunn in Thailand while his band was on tour." He repeated what Jimmy Earl had told him about the hospital conversation, and his theory that Eon Harbor might have threatened to use the incident against the elder Gunn and then the rock star.

"That sounds a little farfetched. Why would they go to such lengths about a lawsuit?"

"The value of the resort is almost $150 million. They stood to lose half of it. An environmental engineer told Gunn's grandfather that someone had approached him about providing a report without ever looking at the land where the resort is now built, showing that it was contaminated."

Ringo gave him a stare and a raised eyebrow. "Who's this environmental engineer?"

"A guy named Blake Owen."

Scratching his head, Ringo said, "Yeah, well, I guess $75 million is a pretty good motive, but how does that link up with my murder case."

"Whoever killed Riley knew the cameras would be turned off and followed Hess in. Hess might've been in on the murder, but probably not. He was killed so he couldn't talk about it."

Ringo just nodded, opened his folder, and picked up the first sheet. "Okay, here's the report from the CSIs on the Hess crime scene. I'll give you the gist. No prints were found there except the victim's. The bullet was a 9mm. They think all the blood probably belonged to the victim, but they sent samples to the lab for analysis. A large quantity of drugs was found in the closet, and he had plenty of cash in his wallet, so we know it wasn't a robbery." He picked up another sheet. "The ME says Hess died around 5:00 a.m., which would be in the same time frame as Gunn's murder."

"Did he look at the trajectory of the round?"

"Yes. Based on the angle of the wound and where the slug went into the wall, he said the shooter was probably taller than Hess's five-ten."

That reminded Dalton that the ME had said the same thing about Gunn's shooter. In both cases the killer would be taller than six feet.

SIX

"WHERE'VE YOU BEEN?" Crook asked as Dalton returned to the office.

"I met with Jack Ringo. Didn't help much, though. You have a few minutes?"

"Sure." They found an empty conference room and closed the door.

Dalton opened his notepad. "The killer of Gunn and Hess is over six feet tall. Vici and the men I've seen at Eon Harbor don't fit that description."

Crook shrugged. "They could've hired somebody to do it."

Nodding, Dalton said, "Yeah, they could. Both kill shots resembled professional hits and were probably accomplished with the same 9mm weapon. But something about that bothers me. I wonder how Hess would've known a hit man, and was chummy enough to let him follow him home after killing Gunn."

"Did they find Hess's phone?"

"No, the phone was missing, just like Gunn's. Too bad. It might've shown contact with the killer. We found Hess only because Colin Casey told us about him. Otherwise, he might've lain in that house until the snake ate him up."

Crook shivered. "Maybe that's what the killer had

in mind. I don't think the snake opened the cage on his own."

Frowning, Dalton said, "We just don't have much to go on. Have you heard anything from the CSIs?"

"No, nothing yet."

Dalton called Tarver and put the phone on speaker. "What's the status on DNA from the Gunn murder?"

"I got the results back a few minutes ago. All the blood at the scene turned out to be the victim's, and it matched the blood on the steering wheel of the stolen car. No other DNA was found in either place. I'll send you an email when I finish going over it."

He had hoped for more, but got about what he expected. Professionals didn't leave DNA behind, at least not their own. "Okay, thanks." They hung up.

"So it's confirmed," Dalton said. "Jimmy Earl's car was involved, either used by Earl himself, or stolen by someone wanting to frame him. Earl needed the money from the insurance proceeds, so he had a million-dollar motive, but if he did it I don't understand how his battery cable got loosened. We need to get him in here."

Dalton phoned Earl and asked him to come into the office.

"I thought you were done with me," Earl said.

"We just have a few more questions." He didn't want to alarm him and have him take off.

Earl relented, said he could be there in fifteen minutes.

After Dalton got to his desk, Lieutenant Springer hurried over. "I got an email from Tarver about the DNA. It was the victim's blood in the stolen car. You need to arrest Jimmy Earl."

"I'm pretty sure somebody tried to frame him."

"Are you kidding? I want you to pick him up."

Dalton felt his face flush. "Have you taken over the investigation, Lieutenant?"

Springer gave him a smirk. "Well, I am your supervisor."

Nodding, Dalton wanted to tell him to back off, or else, but thought better of it. "I just called Earl and asked him to come in."

"When was that?"

Dalton glanced at the time on his computer. "Twenty minutes ago."

"Then he's probably running. Better put out a BOLO."

"Yeah, I'll get right on that." As he stared at the lieutenant, the phone rang. The display indicated it was the desk sergeant, and he pressed the speaker button to answer.

"This is Duffy out front. You got a visitor. Man named Jimmy Earl."

"Okay, I'll come get him." He left Springer standing there with a look of disappointment on his face.

Dalton retrieved Earl, stopped by Crook's desk, and the three went to an interrogation room. When they sat and turned on the recorder, Dalton told Earl about the blood in his car.

"You have to believe me, it was stolen." Perspiration beaded on the drummer's face. His eyes darted between the two detectives.

"If that's the case," Dalton said, "How do you explain somebody getting your keys?"

"I don't know. They were hanging on a hook in my

kitchen. The housekeeper and some girlfriends were the only ones who could've taken them. But I don't think they would've killed Riley."

"We need their names."

Earl took a deep breath and let it out. "Okay, give me something to write on."

Crook tore a sheet of paper from his notepad and handed it to him, along with a pen. "Include phone numbers and addresses, if you know them."

Shaking his head, Earl twisted his mouth to the side and wrote. When he finished, he handed over the list. His penmanship looked like that of a third-grader.

Glancing over it, Dalton said, "How well did you know these women?"

"I've known a couple of them for a while. The others I just met recently."

"Which ones would know about Wilbur Hess?"

Earl ran his fingers through his hair. "Aw, man." He sighed. "I don't know." After a few seconds he took the list and put a mark by two names. "Wilbur came over while those two were there."

"When was that?" Dalton asked.

"The day before Riley's party."

"So one of them could've taken the keys while you were out of the room?"

"Yeah, I guess."

"What about Wilbur? Could he have taken the keys?"

Earl's eyes widened. "I forgot about him. I left him in the kitchen and went to the bedroom for some cash. He took the keys. He had to."

That made sense. It could mean he was in on the plan

from the beginning, but might not have known how it would end up.

"Was there any bad blood between him and Riley?"

The drummer shook his head. "Hmm, no, not really."

"Sounds like you're hedging."

"Well, back when he was our roadie, Riley treated Wilbur like dirt. I'm sure he didn't forget it."

So Wilbur had a motive for getting even with the rocker.

"Okay, what did he have against you that would cause him to steal your car and set you up for a frame?"

"I've been thinking about that for the past few minutes. He and I got along okay. I once chewed him out for puncturing one of my drumheads with a mic stand while we were on tour. I had to scramble to get another one in time for the concert."

"That's it? He broke your drum?"

Shrugging, Earl said, "It's the only run-in I can remember."

"Did you buy a lot of cocaine from him?"

Earl cut his eyes away. "Spent nearly everything I made during an eight-month stretch."

"Did you owe him any money?"

"Yeah, I owed him about eleven grand."

"You think he could've taken your Camaro because of the debt?"

The rocker's eyes widened. "Huh, I hadn't thought of that."

"Do Casey and Sheffield know about the incident in Thailand that you related to me?"

"Maybe. I wasn't exactly Riley's confidant. I just happened to pick him up at the hospital, and he was still shook up and babbling. He probably told Colin. They were pretty thick."

"They were good friends?"

"I don't know if you'd call them good friends, but Riley probably talked to him more than the rest of us because they were the first two members of the band. A number of others came and went. Then me and Sheffield joined about the same time, and we've been with them close to ten years." Earl seemed to realize he had used the present tense and shook his head. "I don't know what's gonna happen now. It won't be Redgunn without Riley."

"Everybody should be pretty well set with the insurance proceeds."

Shrugging, Earl said, "Well, yeah, for a while. Won't last long, though."

"You just talking about yourself or the others, too?"

"None of us have anything put back. I heard Colin is deep in debt, like me."

When Dalton had spoken with Colin Casey, he said he earned over a million on the tours, and even more on record sales.

"What about record sales? Casey said you guys earn millions in royalties."

Earl huffed a laugh. "Yeah, right. Record sales have tanked over the last few years. Riley was hoping to put together a deal with two brothers from Canada to produce a new album. But that's out, now."

It sounded as if Casey had misled them about his need for the insurance proceeds. That might warrant another talk with the guitarist.

"Tell me about Eon Harbor."

The drummer's brow furrowed. "Eon Harbor? You mean the hotel?"

Hotel? Dalton went along to see where it would lead. "Yeah, the hotel."

"That's where we stayed in Thailand while we were there on tour."

"How did it happen that you stayed there?"

"You'd have to ask Wilbur. Well, if he wasn't dead. He made all the reservations for us."

"You know anything about Douglas Vici, the attorney?"

Earl shook his head. "Never heard of him."

"Okay, back to Wilbur. When did he start dealing and stop being your roadie?"

"It was right after we got back from Thailand. We concentrated on songs for another album, and didn't really need him."

They finished up a few minutes later. As Crook walked Earl toward the front, Springer came out of the adjacent room where he had been watching through the one-way glass. He scowled at their guest, but didn't say anything until they were out of earshot.

"Why are you letting him go?" Springer asked.

"He didn't kill Gunn."

"All the evidence points to him."

"No, it doesn't."

Crook came back and Springer said, "Do you agree with your partner on letting that guy go free?"

Dalton saw fear in Crook's eyes as he said, "Yeah, we don't think he did it."

The lieutenant said, "You better be right," and stomped off toward his office.

When he had gone, Crook said, "Are we gonna get in trouble over this?"

Dalton grinned. "Don't sweat it. The only way we'll be in trouble is if we don't identify that killer pretty soon." He went to his desk and phoned Jack Ringo.

"We just talked with one of the members of the Redgunn band. He said they stayed at the Eon Harbor Hotel when they were in Thailand, and Wilbur Hess arranged it for them. The Eon people did something to Riley Gunn while he was in Thailand, and Hess was part of it."

Ringo remained quiet for a few beats, and then said, "You sure it's the same group that owns the Key West Star?"

"Yes, no way it's a coincidence. From all I gather, Hess was just an errand boy for the band, and Eon probably made him a better deal. He started dealing drugs right after the band arrived in Key West. I think the Eon guys had something to do with that, too."

"Still sounds pretty farfetched to me. Hess was a drug dealer. They deal with bad people, and they die every day. It doesn't take a conspiracy to get them killed."

"Okay, I'll buy that. Were you able to get Hess's call record from his wireless carrier? He probably had conversations with whoever killed him."

"We don't have that yet, but I'll check it out." He hung up.

The dial tone droned in Dalton's ear. So much for comparing notes. Maybe Ringo had too much on his plate. Or maybe he just wasn't all that interested in solving a drug-dealer's murder. Dalton knew somebody who could get Hess's call history, but it wouldn't be legal, and if anybody found out it would probably get him fired. Still, he'd keep that in the back of his mind in case Ringo became uncooperative.

It was too bad he hadn't been able to stay longer at the Hess crime scene before the KWPD arrived. He wondered if he could get in there without being noticed. A drive-by might tell him if any uniforms were posted nearby.

On his way out, he stopped at Crook's desk. "You playing at the club tonight?"

Crook smiled. "Yeah, and the Friday crowd should be even bigger than last night."

"Okay, I'm gonna go check on some things. See if you can find any more stories about Eon Harbor. According to what Earl told us, they were probably responsible for what happened to Gunn in Thailand. The lawsuit between the elder Gunn and the owners of the Key West Star was probably in full swing, and they were looking for a way to get the old man to back off. They would have known about Redgunn and the Asian tour, so they offered Hess a deal on the hotel. He probably didn't know what they had in mind at that point, and maybe never knew. It's my guess that Eon's attempt at blackmail didn't work on the grandfather or Riley, so they chose plan B."

Crook nodded. "Okay, I'll do some more research."

"Another thing, see if you can get some information on Colin Casey's financial status. He led us to believe he was pretty well set, but Jimmy Earl seemed to think he needs money."

Crook glanced at the time on his computer. "I have to leave by five. The band'll crank up at happy hour."

"Yeah, well, do what you can." Dalton gave him a wan smile and headed out.

As he reached his car, his phone rang. Lola Ann. "Hey, how's it going?"

"Okay," Dalton said. "How about you?"

"Everything's great. You want to get drinks and dinner later?"

The time on the dash showed a few minutes past 4:00 p.m., and he had already been running for twelve hours, with just a few hours' sleep before that. He yawned. "When did you have in mind?" She probably wanted information about the Gunn murder, and he didn't mind giving her some of the details. She might help him later if he needed it.

"How about seven?"

"Yeah, sounds good."

They decided on a place and hung up. He drove to Hess's home and didn't see any police cruisers, but residents were out in their yards working on boats and tending shrubbery, and a woman was walking a small dog. Too many eyes to get into the place without being seen. After dark would be better.

Crook called and said he'd found something on Colin Casey. "He bought a waterfront estate for $6 million."

"When was that?"

"Couple of weeks ago."

"That's interesting. What about his finances?"

"I did a credit check, and he owes a lot of money. Mostly credit card debt. Maybe that's what Jimmy Earl was talking about. His rating isn't bad, though, so he must be keeping up with it."

"It's been a long day, so I'm heading home. Let's get him in tomorrow morning and talk to him about it."

Crook remained silent for a couple of seconds, and then said, "You're working tomorrow?"

"Yeah, aren't you?"

His partner sighed. "I guess so. What time?"

"Set him up for ten."

"Okay, roger that. See you then."

Dalton rolled into the marina a half-hour later and went to his cottage. Cupcake came in through the pet door and greeted him with a nuzzle to the knee and a purr. He wanted attention, maybe to go for a walk. Dalton felt too tired, so he placated him with a can of tuna.

A few minutes after falling into bed, he dropped off to sleep. It seemed like only a few minutes had passed when his alarm woke him two hours later. He showered, brushed his teeth, and headed out to meet Lola Ann.

As he left, Eric said from the deck. "I saw your car and figured you'd crashed. You going back out?"

"Yeah, there's something I need to do. It'll be late when I get back."

LOLA ANN STEPPED out of the car when he pulled in next to her. She looked as radiant and beautiful as ever.

"Right on time," she said.

The sun was still up and would make the outside deck a scorcher, so they went into the restaurant bar and got a table in the corner. After they gave the waiter their drink orders, she said, "I heard you're investigating the Riley Gunn murder."

He grinned. "You heard right."

"You weren't going to tell me, you sneak."

"I would've told you, when the time was right."

"Yeah, after everybody else ran the story."

"I gave you some pretty good stories a few months ago."

She reached over and patted his hand. "Yes, you did. Anything you can tell me now, about Riley Gunn?"

Dalton shook his head. "Probably no more than you already know. He had a party the night he was killed, and we've interviewed everyone who attended. They all have alibis."

"What about the drummer, Jimmy Earl. A source told me you found his car near the crime scene, and it had the victim's blood on the steering wheel."

He stared for a moment, his face heating up. "Who told you that?"

"Sorry, I can't reveal my sources."

Dalton wondered if someone in the sheriff's office or the Key West PD had told her. It could be any of a number of people, but the first person who came to mind was Springer. He had insisted on arresting Earl not long before Lola Ann called.

When he didn't say more, she continued, "Well, you going to tell me about Earl, or not?"

He gave her a mocking smile. "Maybe your source will tell you."

"Hey, don't be that way." She reached for his hand again and squeezed it.

He pulled away. "I know you have a job to do, and I'll let you know when I have something you can use."

The drinks arrived, and he took a long slug from his beer bottle. It felt good going down his parched throat.

"I can't tell you my source because I don't know who he is. A guy called out of the blue and wouldn't give me his name. The caller ID showed up as 'Unknown.'"

Dalton nodded. Maybe he had overreacted. He didn't like it, but it wasn't her fault. They ordered dinner, a shrimp salad for her, and grilled grouper for him. She had another drink, but he declined. Conversation remained light, the news of the anonymous source still on his mind. Maybe he would feed some information to Springer and see if it ended up with Lola Ann…or maybe he was just being paranoid. Later, in the parking lot, she invited him to her place.

"Maybe another time. There's something I need to do."

Giving him a pouty smile, she said, "Okay, I'll hold you to that." Her glistening eyes were like magnets in the glow of the streetlamps. She knew how to get what she wanted, but it wouldn't work that night.

He headed back to Key West and to Hess's house. There still were no police cars anywhere to be seen, and the residents seemed to have all headed inside. After parking in the driveway of a home with a Sale sign in the yard, he headed down the block and to the dead drug dealer's back door. He stretched on gloves, peeled back crime scene tape, and picked the lock.

Inside, he felt his way through the kitchen using his phone for light, and glanced at the cage in the corner, glad the snake was gone. The place was an even bigger mess since the police had gone through it. He eased down the hall to the bedroom and to the closet. As expected, the bag of drugs was gone. Several boxes and pairs of shoes lay scattered. Down on his knees, he moved the debris out of the way and looked for any cracks in baseboard or cuts in the carpet. There didn't seem to be any, so he stood and checked the inside walls and the ceiling, but didn't find anything there, either.

He went to the bedside table, pulled open drawers, and found only porn mags. Back in the hall, he noticed a door at the end. Inside he found shelves for linens, but no linens, just a lot of junk Wilbur had crammed inside. As with the bedroom closet, he checked around the floor and walls. There were no loose boards and no openings in the wall. Closing the door, he sighed and turned back toward the kitchen, wondering where Hess might hide something he didn't want to be found. A cheap reproduction hung on the wall, and he checked behind it but found only a nail for hanging.

There had to be some hiding place. Hess dealt in drugs, an illegal activity, and would have had secrets to be guarded. Back in the bedroom closet, he went over it again and still found nothing. Inside the linen closet, he splashed the light on the ceiling. Something appeared unusual about it, and he found a chair, dragged it close, and stood on it. Comparing it with the hall ceiling, it was a few inches lower. About two foot square, the piece of painted board rested on molding around its edges. It lifted easily, and he was able to push it up between the joists and out of the way. The original ceiling had been cut out and replaced with the removable one. Reaching up into the cavity on the far side, he felt a metal box. When he pulled it down and opened it, he found stacks of cash and a phone.

SEVEN

AFTER A LATE breakfast the next morning, Dalton drove to the office, pondering what he should do about the phone in Hess's linen closet. He had turned it on and found it password protected. Something was on it that Hess didn't want discovered or he wouldn't have locked it and hidden it with his cash. Dalton gave up and put it back. Because of the way he'd found it, he wouldn't be able to use sheriff's resources to unlock it. If he got someone else to do it, he wouldn't be able to use any evidence on it against a murder suspect, at least not in any legal proceedings.

Since it was Saturday, the office was mostly vacant when Dalton arrived. Colin Casey was already there with Crook in an interrogation room. After thanking their guest for coming in, Dalton flipped on the recorder and cited the date and time and those present. "Okay, Mr. Casey, the reason we asked you here is to clear up a discrepancy. During our initial conversation with you I mentioned the life insurance proceeds from Riley Gunn's policy. You said you didn't need the money because you earned more than that on tour and even more on record sales. Since we spoke with you, we've learned that you are deep in debt and the band's record sales are not so rosy. What do you have to say about that?"

Casey's nerves seemed on edge. His hands shook,

eyes darted. Maybe just a bad hangover. "Well, uh, I really don't remember saying anything about my financial situation."

"This is what I wrote down: 'I make a lot more than a million dollars when we're on tour. And my share of record sales are even more than that.'"

"Huh. Well, I guess if you wrote it down…"

The detectives stared and waited for him to say more. Finally, Casey said. "I guess I was exaggerating." He tried for a smile that didn't quite pan out. "And I didn't want you to think I killed Riley for his insurance."

"Can I see your phone?"

The guitarist hesitated before answering. "Uh, yeah, I guess so." He pulled it from his pocket and handed it over. Dalton scanned the call history, looking for Hess's number. It appeared a couple of times over the past week, incoming and outgoing, along with Riley Gunn's. He expected to see Gunn's number, since they were band members. He handed the phone to Crook.

"Did you hear that Wilbur Hess was murdered?"

"Yeah, I did. That's too bad." He didn't appear upset about it at all.

"We think whoever killed Gunn, killed Hess, too."

"What makes you say that?"

"Riley called him several times during the party, and then again not long before he died. Also, the murders are similar. Same caliber weapon, both shot in the head within minutes of each other…and both done by a person about your height."

"Are you accusing me of murdering them?" Casey leaned back and crossed his arms.

Ignoring the question, Dalton said, "How did you expect to pay for the house you just bought?"

Casey shrugged. "I thought the band was on the upswing. We were working on songs, and Riley had the brothers come in from Canada to talk about an album."

"Okay, then, what do you know about Eon Harbor?"

"You mean the hotel in Thailand?"

"Yes. Do you remember what happened there with Riley?"

"I just remember he wanted to leave in a hurry. He never said why. I was a little miffed, because we had to refund a lot of concert tickets."

Dalton checked his notes, and the dilemma of Hess's phone came back to mind. He wondered what could be on it that might break the case.

"You have anything else?" Crook asked.

Shaking his head, Dalton said, "No, I think that covers it, for now." They returned Casey's phone and Crook took him to the front door. When he returned, Dalton said, "When we were at the Hess house, you mentioned something about a Key West PD flap over a deputy's handling of evidence. Can you give me the details on that?"

"I can tell you what I remember. Let's go to my desk." When they were seated, Crook said, "It was a convenience store robbery. The guy came in and demanded the cash in the register. He probably thought the place was empty, but a customer from the rear of the store saw what was happening. He tried to intervene and got shot. The robber got the money and left. The guy didn't die, but they never identified the shooter. The store was located inside the Key West city limits, but the police department had too many cases going on and their CSIs were spread thin. The sheriff sent in our crew to help. One of the police CSI's took a photo of a shell casing, but the casing went missing. Ringo stood by his people and accused our guys of losing it. He said they might've gotten a print from it. Nobody ever found the brass."

"What do you think happened to it?"

Shrugging, Crook said, "All I know is our CSIs are pretty meticulous."

"Could the Key West guys have misplaced it?"

"That's my guess. The sheriff didn't want to make waves, so she told us to stand down. Why are you asking about that?"

"Ringo didn't show me much in the way of evidence that they gathered. Maybe they gave it the broad brush, since Hess was a known dealer."

"Yeah, I can see them doing that."

"You have Ringo's office number handy?" Dalton pulled out his phone.

"Yeah, hold on. He might not be in today, since it's Saturday." Crook gave him a narrow-eyed glance before picking up a laminated sheet from the corner of his desk and reading off the number.

Dalton punched it in. Ringo answered. "This is Dalton. We're opening our own investigation of the Hess murder. This is a courtesy call to let you know we'll be going into the crime scene in a couple of hours. Have someone bring the key so we won't have to break open the door."

Ringo hesitated, then said, "I'm not approving that."

"That's okay, we have the authority to investigate the

murder. As a matter of fact, I'll need a copy of every-thing in your murder file. Have it ready and I'll stop by around five and get it." Dalton hung up.

Crook grinned. "Man, he's gonna hate that."

"I'll say."

Dalton called Tarver on his cell and told him what he needed. Tarver didn't want to round up his crew on a Saturday, but he agreed and said the team would ar-rive by 1:00 p.m.

After hanging up, he thought about something that had been nagging him. Crook had spoken with one band member that Dalton hadn't seen yet. "You said Shef-field, the other band member, had a solid alibi, right?"

"Yeah, pretty solid. He and his girlfriend were at his condo, and they backed up each other's story about when they got home after the party. Both said they'd stayed there all night and they looked still in the bag."

"We have a while before the CSI team shows up. Maybe we should go see Sheffield again."

Crook shrugged, as if he thought it might be a waste of time, but called and found the man at home. After a couple of minutes going back and forth with him, he hung up. "He said we're spoiling his weekend, but he agreed for us to come over."

Fifteen minutes later they sat in the living room of Alan Sheffield's condo. It overlooked the Gulf of Mex-ico. Sheffield, a tall man dressed in a pair of jeans and a T-shirt, had tattoos up his arms and on his neck. He offered them a drink. Crook accepted a bottle of water. When Sheffield came back from the kitchen, he also brought a drink of his own. It looked like whiskey on the rocks. "I hope you don't mind," he said, gesturing with the glass. His words had a hint of a slur.

"Sure, that's fine," Crook said.

They sat on the sofa, and Sheffield said to Crook, "I thought we were done with this. We told you, Richelle and I were here together all night."

A few seconds later a woman came from the hallway wearing a see-through nightgown with very little underneath. "Somebody talking about me?" She had a drink in her hand and slurred her words.

"Get some clothes on," Sheffield snapped at her. "These are police detectives."

Her face twisted into a frown. "Well, I'm sorry I'm such an embarrassment." Her tone sounded anything but sorry. She turned and staggered back the way she had come. Crook's eyes followed her all the way.

When she had gone, Sheffield said, "Sorry about that. I forgot to tell her you were coming by."

Richelle didn't seem in any condition to alibi anybody at the present.

"I have some other questions," Dalton said.

"Sure, shoot." He swigged from his glass, drinking about half of it down.

"Did you know about the insurance policy Riley Gunn took out for the band?"

"Yeah, he told us all about it. I didn't care about it myself. I figured if something happened to him we could still do okay as a band and I wouldn't need that money." His slur was more pronounced. He took another drink.

Colin Casey had said Sheffield was always after Gunn about singing his own songs. "I heard you had an argument recently with Riley Gunn over a song you wanted to record."

"Yeah, I guess you could call it an argument. He told me no dice without hearing me out. I made a fuss, but cooled down a little later. Who told you that?"

"It isn't important. Maybe you cooled down, but didn't forget it. Did you go back to his house after the party to settle the score?"

"What?" His eyes widened. "I told you already, Richele and I came here and didn't leave." He took a big slug from his glass.

Dalton stared for a couple of beats, then said, "Did she continue to drink after you two got here?"

"No, she was fine. We went to bed and went to sleep."

After making some notes, Dalton said, "Okay, tell me about Eon Harbor."

Sheffield's face twisted into a scowl, and he hesitated before saying, "Eon Harbor? What do you mean?"

"What do you know about it?"

"Never heard of it."

"You never heard of it? Do you remember what happened in Thailand?"

The rocker took another drink. "Yeah, we came back early because Riley got sick."

"You remember where you stayed while you were there?"

Sheffield paused, and then shrugged, maybe realizing he was about to be caught in a lie. "Yeah, it was a hotel, that's all I remember."

Dalton nodded. "Okay, that's all I have for now. You have any questions, Detective Crook?"

Crook shook his head, and they got up and left.

Back in the car Crook said, "You think he was telling the truth?"

"No, he's holding back on something. We need to get him and Richelle into the office when they're sober and know they're being recorded. We might find a crack in their story."

They headed on to Wilbur Hess's house and pulled up to the curb. Tarver's van waited in the driveway, and a police cruiser sat on the opposite side of the street. A policeman got out of the car and stepped over as Dalton and Crook got out.

"Detective Ringo asked me to let you in the house."

"Good. I'll need you to leave the key with me, or bring me a duplicate, in case we need to return later."

The cop gave him a questioning look. "I'll have to ask Ringo about that."

"You do that. Please open the place up first."

The officer strode across the front yard, unlocked the door, and headed back to his car. Tarver and his crew went inside, followed by Dalton and Crook.

"Okay," Dalton said to the group, "the Key West PD has already scoured this place, but they didn't find much. I want you to go about it as if they hadn't been here. I want you to look for prints and any DNA, but we also need to search for places Hess might've hidden records or documents, anything that might tell us who he's been dealing with. Look inside all the outlets and air vents, around all the baseboards and in the closets. Also check behind pictures on the wall."

Tarver gave him a condescending stare. "Anything else?"

Dalton smiled. "No, that should do it."

An hour or so later one of the CSIs said, "I think I've got something." Dalton, Crook, and Tarver stepped to the hallway where the investigator stood on a chair in the door of the linen closet. "This is a false ceiling, and it's loose."

"See what's behind it," Tarver said.

"Yeah, there's something here, feels like a box." He got down with the box in his hands, set it on the chair, and opened it. "I think we found his stash." Pulling out stacks of cash and thumbing through the bills, he said, "Must be twenty or thirty thousand here. And there's a phone."

Tarver picked up the phone and turned it on. When it booted up, he said, "It's locked. We need a password to open it. Go back through the house and see if you find anything that looks like a password, but count the money first."

Crook watched as the CSI counted the cash, then recorded the amount on a piece of paper, signed it, and put it inside the box.

They searched for another hour before giving up. As they packed up their equipment and headed out, Tarver said to Dalton, "We'll get one of our techies to look at the phone."

When they exited the house, the policeman with the key got out of the car and met Dalton with a duplicate. He turned without saying anything and left.

Dalton took Crook to his car and headed over to the KWPD. The desk sergeant called Ringo and he came out and took him back to his desk. "So, did you find anything?"

"We got some prints and blood samples that'll probably turn out to be the same ones your guys got. But we also found where Hess kept his cash and there was a phone. It was locked, and our techs are going to work on it. Might be nothing, but we'll find out."

"Where'd you find the cash?"

"In the attic space above the linen closet. Hess had fixed the ceiling so he could take it out and hide his stash up there."

Ringo sighed. "Huh, we missed that. I'll be sure to tell the CSIs about it. They need to be more thorough. You going to share what you find on the phone?"

"You bet, soon as we can get it open."

"Okay, I've got the copies ready for you." He picked up a file folder and handed it over. "I hope you'll do the same with what you find."

Dalton told him he would and headed out the door. At the office, he glanced over the file and spotted something he didn't expect.

EIGHT

ONE OF THE pages in the murder file Ringo had given Dalton was an arrest report dated ten days prior. Hess and Riley had fought outside Hess's home around midnight and a neighbor called 911. When officers arrived, both men gave them lip and got arrested for disturbing the peace. The charges were dropped the next morning.

About a week later, both were dead.

Dalton wondered why they were fighting and called Gunn's attorney Hilda Wright. When she answered he asked if she knew about the altercation.

"Yes, I heard."

"You know why they were fighting?"

"No, Riley never said. Even if I knew, I couldn't tell you. Client confidentiality."

"Your client is dead."

"Doesn't matter. I can be sued by his family if I disclose something that brings them embarrassment."

He wondered if she really didn't know, or was just stonewalling. "This could be important. You sure you don't know what it was about?"

"Sorry, I don't." She hung up.

He did a computer search on Riley Gunn, wondering if the incident had made the news. Lots of links popped up, but he didn't see anything pertaining to a fight. Many of the items referred to social media accounts. Dalton opened one of them and found it to be a page for the band. It provided some history, including when they had formed and their early works. Not much had been posted in the last year, and those prior were posts advertising albums and concerts. Some were videos. Since Dalton had never heard any of their music, he opened one from a concert in Germany several years before. Riley strutted across the stage as he belted out a rock song, his voice a mixture of gravel and blues, his long hair flipping with the beat. Dalton understood the source of his stardom: his presence had total command of the stage. The camera rarely panned to Casey, Earl, or Sheffield, even though the guitars and drums seemed as good as those in any top band. In the rare moment when the lens found them, each seemed to be in a world alone, maybe accustomed to living in the background. Watching the video gave him a heightened awareness for what would happen to the group without Riley: each of musicians might develop a niche elsewhere, but Redgunn was finished.

. Another link was Gunn's personal page. It, too, had little activity in the past year. Some posts asked about his future concert plans. Others commented on one of his songs, how it touched them in various ways. He responded with a minimum of words when he responded at all. Going back a couple of years, Dalton spotted a post by a woman named Tara Sand. It read, *I miss you.* Gunn didn't reply to that one.

Dalton clicked on Tara's name and brought up her page. She appeared to be in her thirties, a striking woman with dark hair, large blue eyes, and a mesmerizing smile. He lingered on the photo for a moment before clicking on her background. It revealed that she lived in Islamorada. There were no photos of family members or friends, the page consisting only of a few posts each year. As he scrolled through them, he thought he might be wasting time, putting off heading home, until he spotted a photo from four years earlier. The image pictured a younger Tara, maybe in her late teens or early twenties, standing next to Riley Gunn. He looked about her age, probably years before he established Redgunn. The sun reclined on the horizon behind them. Another man stood in the background, half turned toward the sun, drinking from a beer bottle that obscured part of his face. She had written, *Hanging out at Mallory Square, a long time ago.*

Dalton thought the photo of her and Gunn must have been special, since it was her only personal one. All other posts shared images and thoughts from her connections, rather than her own. He wondered if the two had reconnected recently, and if she might be the other woman that had come between him and Hilda Wright. He found Tara's number on a search and punched it into his phone. It rang several times without an answer.

SUNDAY CAME AND WENT. Eric had errands for him that consumed most of his day. In the evening, Dalton relaxed on the deck with his uncle, some of the marina guests, and Cupcake. The cougar kept them entertained chasing bugs that buzzed around the tiki torches. Dalton tried Tara Sand's number a couple more times without success.

On Monday morning, Dalton wore a lightweight suit to the office. The ME had released Riley Gunn's body on Saturday, and his funeral was scheduled for 11:00 a.m. Crook saw him as he arrived and said, "You going to court today?"

"No, Riley Gunn's funeral."

Crook just nodded and said, "Oh." He went back to his keyboard, maybe hoping he wouldn't get roped into attending.

Dalton left the office at 9:40 and found a parking spot a block from the church. Perspiration beaded on his forehead and inside his coat as he made his way down the street and entered the vestibule. Being first to arrive, he took a seat on the back row. Mourners began entering a few minutes later. By 10:30 the room was completely filled. Tara Sand hadn't been among those in attendance. Then, a few minutes before the service began, he saw her peek around the corner, searching for a place to sit. She looked stunning in a black dress. He stood, eased over to her and said, "Take my seat."

Giving him a wary smile, she whispered, "Thank you," entered, and sat down.

Dalton waited in a chair in the corner of the vestibule. When the service ended, Tara came out first and hurried toward the door. He stood and headed over to her.

"Ms. Sand, I'm a detective with the sheriff's office investigating Mr. Gunn's death. Can I have a few minutes of your time?" He held up his badge for her to see.

She frowned, mopped tears from her face, and said, "Okay, I guess."

When they stepped outside, he told her they could talk in his car. "It's right here on the street."

As they got in, she said, "Can we get away from here?"

"Sure, where are you parked?"

"It's several blocks down on the right."

He pulled into traffic ahead of the crowd. "I saw a photo on social media of you and Riley from a long time ago and wondered if you've spoken with him recently."

She began to cry. Between sobs, she said, "We went out a couple of times the week before he died."

"Did you know about the party at his home?"

"Yes, he told me it was mostly a business party and would be boring for me."

Dalton nodded. "His band members, some record producers, and his lawyer. Do you know his lawyer?"

"You mean Hilda?"

"Yes, Hilda. According to her, she and Riley had a thing, but he busted up with her over someone else. Was that you?"

She nodded and began crying again. "I thought we were finally going to be together."

After a protracted silence, as her sobs abated, he said, "Do you know anyone who wanted to do him harm?"

"No. I've been thinking about that since it happened. Why would anyone want to kill Riley?"

Several reasons came to mind, but he didn't think this was the time to share his suspicions. Maybe she didn't know the man as well as she thought. He apparently treated his band members with little respect, and there didn't seem to be any love lost by any of them. Earl had said Riley treated Wilbur Hess like dirt when he worked for him as a roadie. The lawyer, Douglas

Vici, had threatened him on the part of Raven Gardner or Eon Harbor, maybe both.

It seemed as if Tara had held onto her teenage crush, thinking things would be just as they had when they were young. People change. Being a rock star might change a person. Riley Gunn had seen and done a lot since dating Tara when they were young. He might have wanted a relationship with Tara for a different reason. Maybe he saw it as his salvation from a life of high rolling, parties, and drugs. And maybe it was just her perception of what was happening.

"That's my car up ahead next to the palm."

He found a space in the shade a couple of cars beyond hers and pulled in, leaving the engine running and the air blasting. "Do you know Raven Gardner?"

She frowned. "Sure, she was one of my friends when we were young. Why do you ask?"

"You keep in touch?"

"No. We had a falling out when we were in college. She made a play for Riley."

"I spoke with her last week, and she said he wanted to get back together with her but she wasn't interested. Said she had moved on."

"That's a laugh. They were never together to begin with. He mentioned he saw her recently about his lawsuit. She was flirty, and even invited him to her place for dinner. He thought she still carried a torch, but he said he never cared for her as anything other than a friend."

So there were two sides to the story. If what Riley told Tara was true, Raven Gardner had two motives for murder: a lawsuit, and rejection. She also had sufficient height to have done the shooting.

"Do you know Wilbur Hess?"

"Wilbur? He used to hang around with Riley in high school. Kind of an introvert, as I remember. Riley made fun of him. Why would you ask about him?"

"He was murdered the same night as Riley. The same person probably killed both of them."

"That's a shock. I haven't thought about him in years. I used to feel sorry for him, the way Riley treated him."

"What do you mean?"

"He did lots of things for Riley, probably hoping his popularity would rub off on him. Riley used him like a servant."

"From what I gather, he was still doing that. Hess was the band's roadie, and more recently he became a source for drugs. Riley and at least two other band members bought cocaine from him on a regular basis."

"Huh. I heard Riley almost died last year of an overdose, but he told me he was off the drugs. I guess he had me fooled." She stared out through the windshield, maybe rethinking her relationship with Gunn and remembering more of his dark side, rather than the teenage fantasy she had carried for so long and built up in her mind.

"Riley and Wilbur were arrested about a week before their murder for fighting. Do you know what that was about?"

"No. He didn't mention it to me."

"Okay, if you think of anything that could pertain to Riley's murder, give me a call." He handed her one of his cards.

She got out, and Dalton drove to the office. Not knowing who Riley was seeing before his murder had nagged at him, but now that he knew, it didn't seem to be of any benefit to the investigation. What Tara had said about Hess sounded like a motive for him killing Riley, but someone had murdered him, too.

Springer came out of his office and caught him as he approached Crook's desk. "Where've you been?" the lieutenant asked.

"Gunn's funeral. I wanted to talk with the woman he had been seeing recently. She showed up at the church."

"Did you learn anything new?"

Dalton shrugged. "Not really. She and Gunn went together when they were young, but she'd been out of touch with him for a long time. I got the impression she didn't know much about his current life."

The lieutenant gave him a smirk. "So Jimmy Earl is still the best suspect you have."

They had been through that already. There were good reasons why Earl hadn't been arrested. Dalton glanced at Crook, who picked up his phone and punched in a number.

A second later, the phone rang at Dalton's desk. "I need to get that." He turned and headed toward his workstation.

Springer sighed and stomped away.

"Thanks," Dalton said into the handset.

Crook chuckled. "You bet."

When they hung up, Dalton phoned the officer who had arrested Gunn and Hess for disturbing the peace.

"You remember what they were fighting about?"

The officer paused, then said, "Nah, I just remember they were both three sheets and calling each other names."

"Do you have the address or phone number of the person who called it in?"

"Why do you need this information?"

"I'm investigating the murder of both those guys. What they were arguing about could be important."

"Okay, I'll look it up and call you back."

They hung up, and a few minutes later the phone rang, the officer on the other end. He gave Dalton the address and phone number of the man who had called 911 about the disturbance. Dalton punched in the number. When a man answered, Dalton asked about the fight.

"I don't know what it was about. It was just a lot of noise, late at night. They were calling each other awful names I don't want to repeat." The neighbor sounded elderly, a tremor in his voice.

"You didn't hear a reason why they were arguing?"

"No, like I told you…wait they were arguing about a man. Give me a minute, and maybe I'll remember his name. Hmm. Oh, yeah, it was Ian something."

When the man didn't continue, Dalton said, "Could it have been Eon Harbor?"

"Yeah, Ian Harbor. That's the guy they were yelling about."

NINE

GUNN AND HESS had been arguing about Eon Harbor. Dalton mused over what might have happened as a catalyst for the fight. A year and a half before, the Redgunn band had stayed at the Eon Harbor hotel in Thailand, where someone convinced Riley that he had hurt or killed a woman. Hess had been responsible for the reservations and could have helped set Riley up. Vici, a lawyer and probably a surrogate for Eon, had threatened Riley if he didn't drop the lawsuit against them. The threat probably involved what had happened at the hotel.

The phone they had found in Hess's closet could be the key. Dalton called CSI Tarver. "You figure out how to open that phone yet?"

"No. I just handed it over to the techs this morning. None of them were in on Saturday."

"It could be important, so put some pressure on them."

Tarver paused, then said, "Yeah, okay, but those guys don't report to me."

"Who did you give it to?"

Another pause. "Randy Teal."

"Okay, thanks." He hung up.

He found Teal's office location and number in the address book. The guy's desk was on the second floor, so he took the stairs and found him in the corner of a large room, surrounded by electronic equipment. Teal looked about twenty-five, with shaggy blond hair and thick glasses. He lay back in his chair with his keyboard in his lap staring at a giant computer monitor. When Dalton approached he sat up and gave him a wary look. Dalton introduced himself and asked about the phone.

"Oh, yeah. I'm working on it now, but with this phone, you have only a few tries for a password, and then it locks up. Then you can't unlock it without erasing everything on it and starting over. I know you need whatever is on the phone, so I'm looking into this guy's background to try to figure out his password. But like I said, I'll get only a few tries and it's over."

"You think you can figure it out?"

Teal shrugged. "Maybe. If I can't, I can try the carrier, but they probably can't unlock it without destroying the data, either. The state lab might figure out some kind of backdoor into the device."

"That sounds like it could take a while."

"Yeah, they might have others ahead of you."

Dalton sighed. "Okay, do what you can, but make it quick, and call me if you run into a dead end. I know somebody who might be able to unlock it."

The techie gave him a wary look, as if to say, *I think you're dreaming.*

Later, at Crook's desk, Dalton said, "Have you learned any more about Eon Harbor?"

His partner gave him a questioning glance. "Like what?"

"I asked you on Friday to see what else you could find on them."

"Oh, yeah. I kinda got sidetracked researching Colin

Casey's finances and setting him up for the appointment on Saturday."

"All right, find out what you can. And this time look for William Chan, too. He's the guy running the show in Key West." He told Crook about the argument between the two murder victims concerning the company.

"Their name keeps coming up," Crook said.

"Yes, and I don't think it's a coincidence."

The lieutenant stepped over and said, "Deputies found a dead man at his home a few minutes ago. It looks like a suicide, but you two need to go out and take a look." He gave Crook the information while Dalton got his notepad from his desk.

When they reached the car, Crook said, "You drive and I'll navigate. I know where this is."

"You get the guy's name?"

"Yeah, it's Blake Owen."

"Blake Owen?" Dalton glanced at him. "That's the environmental engineer who was going to testify for the Gunns in their lawsuit. I talked to him last week. When I told him Riley's mother was considering going forward with the case, he said he had changed his mind about giving testimony. I assumed he got scared because Riley got murdered."

"You think he was afraid enough to commit suicide?"

Dalton thought for a moment, then said, "I don't know."

"If not, that means…"

"It means somebody wanted to shut him up."

They reached the address and parked on the street behind a couple of sheriff's cruisers. Key West PD jurisdiction didn't extend that far north, so they probably wouldn't show up. Two deputies sat in one of the cars. Dalton went over and told them to stay there and to not allow the news media or anybody other than law enforcement to enter the property.

The house, which appeared to be an aging pre-fab, sat at the end of a shady street, several blocks from the Gulf. They went inside and found Blake Owen in the living room. He lay back in a recliner with his eyes closed, as if napping. Two deputies stood close to the body. Both had solemn expressions on their faces, maybe wishing they could be somewhere else. An open pill bottle sat on a table next to the chair. It was empty, and its cap lay on the floor, as if snatched off in a hurry. According to the label on the side, it had contained an opioid pain medication prescribed for Owen five weeks prior. The label indicated a quantity of thirty pills. A cocktail glass also sat there with what appeared to be whisky dregs in its bottom.

"Who called it in?" Dalton said to one of the deputies.

"Cora Leach, the next-door neighbor. She said he was supposed to come to her house for dinner last night and didn't show. His car was in the driveway today, but he didn't answer the phone, so she walked around the house and saw him through the window. The medical examiner is on his way."

Dalton called Tarver and explained the situation. "We need your crew to scour this place."

When he got off the phone, the deputy said. "Looks like a simple suicide. He took a bunch of pills."

"Yeah, it might look that way. You and your partner go canvass the neighborhood and see if anybody remembers seeing any strange vehicles in the last couple of days. Don't worry about Cora Leach. We'll talk to her."

The deputy rolled his eyes and walked away.

Dalton checked the front and back doors for any signs of tampering, but didn't find any. The back door had a simple lock, no deadbolt. When the CSIs and the ME arrived, Dalton and Crook went next door.

Cora Leach had silver-hair, wore tortoise-shell glasses, and probably remembered the Eisenhower administration. She invited them in and offered something to drink. Both declined.

When they were seated, Dalton said, "You told the deputy you saw Mr. Owen through his window."

"I saw the pill bottle on the table, and he looked dead. Did he overdose?"

"We're not sure yet. Do you know why he had the pain pills?"

She shrugged. "He twisted his knee a few weeks ago, but I thought he'd gotten over that. He told me he was taking three pills every day for the first week or so." If he started with thirty, that meant he didn't have many left by the day before.

"So you expected him for dinner last night and he didn't show?"

"Yes, I told him to be here at seven. When he didn't come over, I waited thirty minutes before calling. He didn't answer, so I figured he forgot and went somewhere. I got a little steamed, and didn't bother to call him again until a couple of hours ago. He still didn't answer, but I went out and saw his car in the driveway. I knocked on the door a couple of times before

I started thinking something might be wrong, and I walked around the side and looked in the window. He was just sitting there, but he looked strange to me. I had a key, but I didn't want to go in. I gave it to the deputy when he arrived."

"Were you two close?"

"We liked each other's company. I'm a widow, and he came over for a brandy a few times a week. I don't cook much anymore, and this was the first time I invited him for dinner." She sighed. "I have all that food in the refrigerator now."

"Did you see him the day before yesterday?"

"We had drinks on the deck that evening. He left about ten."

"How many drinks?"

Seeming to blush, she said, "We had several."

"You didn't talk with him after that?"

"No. I expected him for dinner the next day."

Dalton asked about seeing any strange cars the night after the drinks.

"I didn't see anybody over there. Of course, the hedge blocks my view, and I can't see his driveway without going around to the street."

"Did he say anything about still being in pain from the knee injury?"

She shook her head. "No. He walked just fine. Didn't even need the cane anymore."

"Okay. The last time you saw him, did he seem down about anything?"

"No…not down. He did seem preoccupied about something, though. When I asked him if anything was wrong, he said, 'No, I think everything is going to be okay now.' He didn't elaborate, and he didn't seem suicidal, if that's what you're getting at."

What he had said to her didn't sound suicidal to Dalton, either. Dalton had spoken with him on Friday, the day before, and Owen had already backed out of testifying. It sounded as if he thought that would keep him safe.

They left and went back to Owen's house. The ME had the body in the van and stood next to his car, about to get in.

"The lady next door said she last saw Mr. Owen at ten Saturday night," Dalton said. He expected a terse response based on his last conversation with the doctor.

Dr. Bragg nodded. "I think he died about 36 hours ago, but I'll know more after I've had a chance to examine him. Tarver said you don't think this is a suicide."

"No. I think he was murdered so he couldn't testify in the lawsuit the Gunns filed against Raven Gardner."

Shrugging, Bragg said, "It certainly looks like suicide, but I'll check him over thoroughly and get you my findings by the end of the day." He reached for the door handle and turned back. "Oh yes, the sheriff dropped by this morning. He speaks highly of you." Bragg actually smiled.

"Thanks for passing that on." He didn't know how it happened that the sheriff had visited and said good things about him, but he was glad he had. It would make his job easier if he and the ME got along.

Tarver said they would be another hour. Without getting in the CSIs' way, Dalton and Crook scanned through the house for anything that might explain Owen's death.

When they came up empty, they headed out. In the car, Crook said, "What do you think happened back there?"

"I'm guessing Owen was buzzed from brandy when he had a visitor. Probably somebody hired by Lawyer Vici or William Chan. You could get in the back door with a credit card. The intruder could've pointed a gun at him and told him to swallow the pills."

"If somebody did that, I don't know how we'd go about proving it."

"Yeah, I'm afraid you're right."

They got a late lunch of tacos and chips at a food truck and ate in the shade of a large oak. When they got back to the office, Dalton found an email from Tarver for their work at the Hess crime scene. Compared with the results from Ringo's file, there was nothing new. Except for one thing: the phone had two sets of finger-prints on it: those of Wilbur Hess and of Riley Gunn. Why would Riley's prints be on it, unless the phone belonged to him? They had to get it unlocked. It seemed the only piece of evidence with any promise.

He went over to Crook's desk, who had also been perusing the CSI email. They discussed the possibil-ity that the phone could have belonged to Riley Gunn, and that Hess probably took it when they went there and killed him.

Crook leaned back in his chair. "Why do you think he hid it in his closet?"

"I'm guessing it has something on it he wanted to save, maybe because it incriminates the person who did the killing."

"Yeah, could be."

"I've been thinking about William Chan's involvement in all this," Dalton said, "and I'm gonna pay him another visit. While I'm gone, how about setting up Sheffield and his girlfriend to come in later today? That is, if they haven't been hitting the sauce again."

"Sure, I can do that. You think it's a good idea talking to Chan? He seems to have some juice around town."

"If I make him mad enough, maybe he'll slip up and show his hand."

Crook shrugged. "Or get you fired."

Dalton drove to the Key West Star Resort where vehicles crammed the parking lot. The only space he found was all the way in the rear, a good quarter mile from the entrance. Perspiration beaded under his shirt by the time he reached the chill of the lobby. He took the elevator to the fourth floor. As he exited, the door to Eon Harbor's suite opened. Jack Ringo and Douglas Vici backed out, still talking with someone inside, presumably William Chan. Dalton eased down the opposite direction and into an alcove. The two stood there another few seconds talking in inaudible tones before heading to the elevator.

Why would Ringo meet with William Chan and Vici? Dalton wondered if he could be involved with the Asian company. With this new development, he decided to forgo confronting Chan. He waited until the elevator doors closed and the car descended before stepping over and pressing the Down button. As he exited in the lobby, Ringo strode out the front door. Vici waited a few seconds before leaving, maybe so he wouldn't be seen with the detective.

Something nagged at Dalton as he got back in his vehicle, started the engine, and got the air blowing.

The thought eluded him, and he pulled out of the lot into traffic, headed back to the office. While the meeting with Chan and Vici could be innocent, it didn't look good. Dalton decided he would keep the incident to himself. He would need something more concrete before accusing a police detective of anything illicit.

He went to his desk and did a computer search on Jack Ringo. Few links popped up, only one a social media account. Dalton accessed it and peered at a photo of Ringo, seemingly from a few years before. His background indicated that he had been with the KWPD for eleven years. He had lots of connections. Dalton scrolled through them, but recognized the name of only one: Raven Gardner. He wondered how long the two had known each other, and if his visit to William Chan could be on her behalf. Dalton had mentioned Vici's alleged threat against Riley Gunn to several people, Ringo and Vici included. It seemed odd for Ringo to meet with Vici and Chan about that.

Backtracking over his notes, he couldn't help but wonder if Ringo might somehow be involved with the murders. He could have known Wilbur Hess from a drug arrest, and might have known Riley, too, but what would be his motivation? As a cop, the relationship with Vici and Chan could be that of a fixer. The visit Ringo had made the week before to chastise Dalton about harassing the company came to mind. He'd said Chan had complained to the Mayor. It seemed strange that he had gotten there so quickly, since Dalton had just left Chan's office about an hour before. Maybe Chan hadn't called the Mayor at all. Maybe he had a direct line to Ringo.

The nagging feeling came back, and Tara Sand's

photo at Mallory Square floated behind his eyes. He accessed her social media page, found the photo, and zoomed in to 300 percent. The image became blurred and grainy, but the man in the background drinking beer and watching the sunset looked a lot like Jack Ringo. The guy was tall and had dark hair, and though slimmer than the current Ringo, the build was similar. Dalton punched in the number for Tara Sand.

She answered this time, maybe recognizing the number from his card. He asked if she knew Jack Ringo. She hesitated, then said. "Why, yes, I know Jack."

"I wondered if he's the person in the background of your photo of you and Riley at Mallory Square."

"Hmm, maybe. Hold on and let me pull it up?" After a few seconds, she said, "Yeah, that's Jack. I dated him a few times when we were in college, but I was hung up on Riley and broke it off. I think this picture was right after that. He still hung around with us. Why do you want to know about him?"

"Just covering bases. Were the two of you ever together later, as a couple?"

She drew an audible breath. "He phoned a couple of months ago, and we went out a few times. Then Riley came back on the scene, and we seemed to pick up where we left off when we were young. I told Jack we didn't have a future together, and he pitched a fit, got drunk, and came by my house. I wouldn't let him in, and he stood outside yelling, calling me and Riley awful names. I'm surprised the neighbors didn't call the police."

"When was that?"

"About three weeks before Riley died." She paused

and then said, "Wait, you think Jack had something to do with Riley's death?"

"I'm just looking for motives. Jealousy is a strong one, but there are some others where Riley is concerned." Dalton paused, and then said, "Has he ever been involved with Raven Gardner?"

"Not to my knowledge. As I recall, he didn't care much for her."

"All right, thanks for the information. If you speak with Ringo, I'd appreciate it if you didn't mention our conversation."

She agreed and they hung up.

Crook called and told him Sheffield and his girlfriend were due at four, which was in twenty minutes. "He assured me they haven't been drinking today."

Dalton reviewed his notes on their visit to Sheffield's condo. He wanted to go over his alibi again and make sure it was solid. Also, the guitarist hadn't seemed to remember anything about Eon Harbor. That seemed odd since the band had stayed in the company's hotel by that name in Thailand.

When their visitors showed up, Crook put them in an interview room and Dalton joined them. He led off with the question about the alibi.

Sheffield shook his head. "I don't know why you keep asking about that. We both went straight home after the party and crashed. We'd been up for about twenty hours and were exhausted. We slept like the dead."

"Is that your recollection, too?" Dalton asked the woman, Richele Graski.

"Yeah, sure. We were zonked."

"Could your friend here have left during the night without you knowing about it?"

Richele frowned. "No, dude, we slept together, and I'm a light sleeper."

"Okay, Mr. Sheffield, when I asked you at your condo about Eon Harbor, you seemed to draw a blank. I'll ask again. What do you know about that company?"

"I don't remember you asking me that, but it seems like we stayed at a hotel by that name somewhere in Asia. Is that what you're talking about?"

When asked about it at his condo, the guy had said he'd never heard of the company. Now he suddenly remembered. He *was* slightly drunk the first time. Dalton supposed that could have caused his lapse, but he didn't think so. "When you were there, did you know what happened to Riley that caused the band to cut the tour short?"

The guitarist leaned forward on the table, his eyes narrowed. "Yeah, he got sick and ended up in the hospital. I didn't buy that business about a stomach ailment. Riley probably overdid it with the drugs. He was bad about that."

"Wilbur Hess was his primary source of drugs. Did you know that?"

Sheffield leaned back, and blinked a couple of times. "Yeah, that was pretty much common knowledge."

"How about you? Did Wilbur sell you drugs, too?"

"Hey, I don't know what you're getting at, but I didn't have a problem like Riley did."

"Did you know that Wilbur Hess was murdered the same day as Riley Gunn?"

"Yeah, I heard about that. Sad. I liked Wilbur."

Sheffield's words sounded sincere, but he also seemed guarded about something. "On the night of the party, Gunn and Casey snorted cocaine in Gunn's bedroom. Did you join in?"

Sheffield frowned. "No, I didn't. You can ask Richele." He turned to her.

She hesitated a beat, then said, "That's right. The only ones I saw going to Riley's bedroom were Riley and Colin."

They talked another few minutes, but Dalton didn't see the interview going anywhere. The alibi was what he had wanted to nail down, and if the two were telling the truth, they had confirmed that. He thanked them for coming in and they left. When he got back to his desk, he noticed his voicemail light blinking. He accessed it and listened to Dr. Bragg say, "You better come over. I have something to show you."

When he entered the autopsy room, Bragg stood next to the table, pulling a cover over Blake Owen's body. "Let's go over to my office." Dalton met him there and Bragg got behind his desk. "I'm halfway through the autopsy, but thought I should let you know about this. Mr. Owen had a large amount of a narcotic in his blood. Enough to put down a horse. He did swallow drugs consistent with the labeling on the empty pill bottle at his home, but two pills were still in his stomach, dissolved but not digested. That told me he died within seconds after swallowing them. It occurred to me that he might have taken more of the drug earlier and decided he needed the last two to do the job, but that didn't seem likely. If you wanted to kill yourself with pills, you would take the whole bottle at once.

So, I looked him over carefully and found bruising around his neck." He punched keys on his computer and turned the monitor so Sam could see. "Here, take a look." It was an image of the neck and upper chest. Small, darkened spots appeared around the neck area. "I think these were made while someone held him from behind." He brought up another image and zoomed in. "This is the back of Owen's neck. The red spot at the edge of his hairline is the injection point for a hypodermic. Around that spot, I found a trace amount of the narcotic that killed him."

Dalton raised an eyebrow. "That means two people were involved. The one who held him and the one who gave him the kill shot."

TEN

As DALTON RETURNED to his desk, the phone rang. He answered, and the voice on the other end said, "Hey, this is Deputy Wilson. I'm the one you told to canvass the neighborhood around Blake Owen's house. I called a couple of times while you were out, but I didn't want to leave a long message on voicemail."

"Did you come up with something?"

"Only one person saw anything out of the ordinary. Might not be worth mentioning, but you wanted to know about any strange vehicles. An old man named Bobby Carson, who lives around the block from Owen's house, said he went out to walk his dog and saw a dark SUV drive by going really slow. This was about eleven, night before last. The vehicle parked in the driveway of the vacant house next door and two guys got out. Carson said he was behind a bush and didn't think they saw him. They didn't say anything that he could hear, and he went back into his home. He said he got to thinking about them, wondering if they were up to no good, and went out about thirty minutes later. The SUV was gone."

"What about a description of the men?"

"Nah, Carson said it was too dark. He couldn't tell me the make of the vehicle, color, or plate number, either."

Wilson gave him the man's address and they hung up. Dalton wondered if William Chan had a dark SUV. He searched the motor vehicles database, found a black Range Rover registered to Chan, and printed the page.

Crook dropped by and said, "I'm heading home."

Dalton gave him a quick rundown on the call from the deputy and on the ME deciding that Blake Owen had been murdered. Crook seemed disinterested, ready to leave. They had already discussed the likelihood that Owen was murdered, and that didn't seem to surprise him.

"Why don't we go over tomorrow and check out that guy's story," Crook said.

"Yeah, sounds good."

There didn't seem any reason to tell his partner he didn't plan on waiting until morning. A few minutes after Crook left, Dalton phoned Jack Ringo.

"Just wanted to alert you about a murder on Stock Island. It's outside your jurisdiction, but I thought you might be interested, since it probably figures into the other murders we've been investigating. A guy named Blake Owen. You might remember that I mentioned him when we were going over the murder files. He's the environmental engineer who planned to testify for the Gunns in their lawsuit against Raven Gardner."

"Yeah, I remember, and one of your deputies told me about Owen when we crossed paths today. He said he thought it was a suicide."

"It looked that way, because Owen took some pills, but the ME found a puncture mark where a narcotic was injected."

Ringo remained silent for a few beats, and Dalton

wondered if the call was just distracting him from something else he had going on, or what he'd said caught the detective by surprise.

"You there?" Dalton asked.

"Yeah, I'm here. Let me know if you find a link to the Hess murder."

Dalton sensed he was about to hang up and said, "I saw you this afternoon at the Star Resort. You were ahead of me and I didn't get a chance to speak."

Ringo paused again, then said, "Must've been around four. I dropped by there to get information for some people I know who're gonna visit later in the week."

"I thought I saw Douglas Vici there with you."

"Douglas Vici. Who's that?"

"Raven Gardner's lawyer. Riley Gunn told his lawyer that Vici threatened him if he didn't drop the lawsuit."

"What're you getting at? You accusing me of something?"

"No. Not yet. I did wonder why you were talking with Raven Gardner's lawyer, though."

Ringo hung up.

Dalton replaced the handset in the cradle wondering what Ringo was up to. Since he lied about the Star Resort, it could mean he was involved in the Gunn and Hess murders. The tall detective could've been the shooter.

He left the office, drove to Blake Owen's neighborhood, and found the address Deputy Wilson had given him. After parking on the street, he examined the area where he thought the dark SUV might have parked, looking for tire treads. When he didn't find any he strode through the back yard to a three-foot-wide drainage ditch. The other side was Blake Owen's back yard. There were shoe impressions in the soft earth. He took photos and called CSI Tarver, hoping he might still be working. Tarver answered.

"This is Dalton. I'm glad you're still there. I'm at a drainage ditch behind Blake Owen's house and there're some shoe prints I want you to check out."

"You mean now?"

"Well, yeah, right now. If it rains tonight they might be gone."

Tarver grumbled but agreed to come over.

Dalton took a page from his notepad, stuck it on a foot-long stick, and used it to mark the spot for the CSIs. He walked to the end of the property where the ground was firm, crossed over the ditch, and headed to Owen's back door. Had he not stopped for the shoe-prints, it would've taken only a couple of minutes to go from his vehicle to the victim's back door. That gave the two men plenty of time to get inside, murder Owen, and get back to their SUV before the neighbor came back out.

When he got back to where his car was parked, he headed next door to an ancient double-wide. It wore a thick coat of glossy white, paint. Plastic flamingos, pelicans, and dolphins dotted the gravel-covered front yard. A frail man with white hair answered Dalton's knock. He flashed his credential. "Are you Bobby Carson?"

"Yeah, that's me, all my life."

Dalton asked about the SUV, and Carson frowned. "I told all that to a policeman earlier today."

"I know. I just need a couple more details."

The man shook his head. "Okay, come on in. I was just about to open a beer. You want one?"

"Thanks, but I'm still on duty."

They went inside and Dalton took a seat on the sofa. A small black poodle eyed him as he sat down. Carson got his beer and sat in a chair across from him. The dog hopped up in the old man's lap.

Carson said, "I don't have to work anymore. Retired from an auto plant up north and bought this place." From the looks of the man, it appeared he had been retired at least three decades. "I assembled all the parts: doors, hoods, engines, lights. And I welded, too. I did it all." His face slackened in a wistful expression, and he took a drink from his beer. "I hear they have robots to do all that stuff now."

"Yes, I've heard that, too."

"All right. You didn't come here to talk about me. What else do you need?"

"The deputy told me you saw two strange men park at the vacant home next door a couple of nights ago. Can you tell me anything about their appearance?"

"No. It was too dark." Carson frowned. "Why are you interested in those guys?"

"I'm investigating a murder."

The man strangled on his beer and coughed for several seconds. When he got things under control, he said, "Who got murdered?"

"A man who lives around the block."

"And you think those two killed him?"

"Maybe."

Carson's eye grew large, as if just realizing that the men he had watched so casually might have been dangerous. "Well, I couldn't identify them, even if you had them in a lineup. Like I said: too dark."

"But you're certain you saw two men?"

"Oh yeah, I'm certain, but I couldn't see their faces." Carson took a long pull on the beer, slapped his chest with the palm of his hand, and began another coughing fit. The dog jumped down and circled the chair a couple of times, whimpering. It finally settled down and lay at the old man's feet.

When the coughing subsided, Dalton said, "Is there anything else you can tell me about the men, like if they were tall, short, fat, thin?"

"Oh, maybe. Let me think. One was tall and one was short, little, I mean. He was the driver. At first I thought he was kid, but a car went by as they passed by the bushes, and lit them up for a split second. I could see they were both grown men, and the little one had something in his hand, like a small tool box. That house has been on the market for a while, and I figured they were there to fix something." He remained quiet for a beat, then said, seemingly to himself, "They couldn't see me because I was behind the bush."

"Did either of them say anything?"

"No. They just got out and eased through the yard."

"You said a car went by and lit them up. You sure you didn't see their faces?"

The old man frowned and took a long slug of his beer. "I'm pretty sure they were looking the other way, and I didn't see their faces, but the big guy had a tattoo on his arm."

"What was the design of the tattoo?"

"Aw, I couldn't tell. Just looked like a lot of ink to me."

Dalton nodded. He didn't think the tattoo helped much. Lots of men had them. The members of the Redgunn band had plenty of ink on their arms, and he didn't think anything about it at the time. It was something to check out, though. Maybe get photos to show Carson.

"Can you remember anything else about the vehicle they were driving?" Dalton asked.

"Just that it was a shiny, dark color. It was quiet, too. I barely heard the engine." Carson stared at the door for a moment, and then said. "You think they might come back and murder me, too?"

"I think you're safe, but keep an eye out for the vehicle. Call me if you see them again." He left one of his cards and went out the door.

In the car, Dalton thought about what the man had said about the intruders' sizes. The small one fit the description of William Chan and his driver. Chan's vehicle also fit the description the man had given of the SUV, but it also fit that of hundreds of other vehicles in the Keys. The larger man could have been the shooter in the Gunn and Hess murders. He wondered if Jack Ringo had tattoos. The detective had worn long sleeves each time Dalton had seen him.

He located Chan's address on the motor vehicle printout and entered it into the navigation system. It indicated Chan lived about three miles away, a block off Flagler Street. The trip took just a few minutes. Chan's house was palatial compared to the retired auto worker's place. A two-story, it sat about a hundred feet from the street. Palms obscured most of the façade. Dalton drove by and parked a block away with a clear view of the driveway.

Twenty five minutes later, Chan's limo turned in. Dalton wished he could get a search warrant and go through the house, but knew he didn't have enough evidence. He wondered how difficult it would be to get inside the place while both men were away, and thought he might consider that for the next day.

As he pulled away from the curb, a black Range Rover exited Chan's driveway and headed the other way. Dalton waited until it got ahead by a couple of blocks and followed. Whoever drove the vehicle could be meeting somebody important to the case. He stayed behind the SUV until it reached the Star Resort. Instead of turning into the employee lot, as the limo had done the week before, it kept going and rolled into the marina next door. A Key West Star Resort sign stood at the entrance. It appeared open to the public, but Dalton supposed it existed primarily for the use of resort clientele. A place for the wealthy yacht owners to park their vessels while lodging in the hotel.

The dash clock read 8:35, and the sun had been gone for a few minutes, leaving the area in twilight. Dalton pulled onto the shoulder of the road and felt in the rear floor for his field glasses. He brought them to his eyes and tracked the SUV. It turned into a spot alongside the dock. A man got out, and Dalton recognized him as the Asian limo driver. He now wore a casual shirt and pants instead of a suit. The driver peered around the marina, as if searching for something, or someone, and then eased down the dock and boarded a fishing boat fitted with tall outriggers.

Dalton drove into the marina, turned right, and circled around so he would be behind Chan's employee when he left the lot. He pulled over to the side before reaching the SUV and turned off his headlights. The area lay in near darkness, and he wondered why the overhead lamps hadn't lighted up.

A few minutes later the SUV driver exited the boat carrying something large. The vehicle's interior light flashed on when he opened the back hatch and loaded the item inside. It was a cooler, the kind that might contain iced-down fish. When he got inside and backed out, a black SUV sped by him and turned inward, blocking his way. Three men wearing DEA vests hopped out and pointed automatic weapons at the Rover's windshield. They yelled for the driver to get out of the vehicle and on the ground. He did as they instructed, and one of the men retrieved the cooler. He nodded to the others and carried it to their vehicle. They cuffed the Asian man and drove away with him in the back seat.

Dalton began to pull out and follow when a small car went by. It was a tan sedan that looked familiar, and when he saw the driver, he remembered where he had seen it: parked at Marilyn Coe's mobile home. From the beginning he had hoped the beauty with purple hair wasn't involved, but being present at an apparent drug transaction didn't look promising. She had an intense expression on her face, and she appeared to be carrying on a conversation with someone not in the car. He pulled out and followed.

A few blocks away from the marina, Coe turned and headed in the direction of the bar where she worked. Dalton stayed back several car lengths and turned into the bar's driveway as she parked in an employee area far away from the entrance. She hurried to the door and went inside.

Soft reggae played on the jukebox as Dalton entered. He didn't see Coe until he reached the bar and she came out from the back. She began serving drinks, and when she spotted him, she smiled and ambled over. "Hey, you off duty, or is this more police work?" If she had been upset before, she had gotten over it, and now seemed as carefree as the last time he had visited the bar.

"Give me whatever you have on tap."

"Coming right up." She went away and returned carrying a frosted mug with a quarter inch head on the beer. "So how's your investigation going?"

"Not good," he said, as he pulled a bill from his wallet and laid it on the bar.

"Uh-oh. You look like you're in a bad mood."

He took a long drink from his mug and set it down. "Yeah, you could say that."

"Anything I can help you with?"

"You might. I just saw you over at the Star Resort's marina. Why don't you tell me what you were doing there."

The smile dropped a few watts. "Must've been somebody else. I've been here a while."

Dalton shook his head. "No, it was you. I also saw the DEA haul away William Chan's limo driver, along with what appeared to be a cooler filled with drugs. You know anything about that?"

Something changed in her eyes, and she said, "Don't go anywhere. I'll be back." She stepped away and went through the door leading to the back. About three minutes later she came out, followed by a man shaking his head, a frown on his face. He went over to serve a customer, and Marilyn came down Dalton's way. She made a drink for a man a couple of seats away. Then, without looking at Dalton, she picked up his money, left a small note, and went back to serving customers down the bar.

The note read, "Meet me at my place in twenty minutes." He palmed it, took a last drink from his beer, and left.

Before that night, he would have been excited about an invitation to her home, but he knew this was different. His pulse beat in his ears. When he reached his car, he got in and waited. She exited a few minutes later and went to her car. He followed.

When they reached her mobile home, she pulled into the small driveway, and he parked on the street. Inside, she said, "Have a seat. You want a drink?"

"What do you have?"

"Gin, vodka, wine."

"Gin and tonic?" He asked as he sat down in an easy chair facing the sofa.

"Sure." She made the drink and handed it to him. "Chill out while I go change clothes. I spilled whiskey on these jeans."

When she left the room, he sipped the drink, and then pulled his service weapon and laid it on his lap. He thought he heard the shower running down the hall. About fifteen minutes passed before she returned wearing the nightgown she had worn the first time he had talked with her. She held something in her hand, but it didn't appear to be a weapon. After making herself a drink, she took a seat on the sofa and laid the object on the table. It was a leather clutch. Her hair looked different, pinned back from her face, and she appeared to have removed all makeup from her face. It didn't diminish her beauty at all. If anything, she looked even more beautiful than before.

"It's been a long day," she said and took a drink from her glass.

"My patience is wearing thin. You going to answer my question about the marina?"

"Yes." Glancing at the handgun in his lap, she said, "Don't shoot me," and then reached for the clutch. She opened it and held it up for him to see. It was a photo of her, only with blonde hair, and above the photo were the words, "Drug Enforcement Agency."

ELEVEN

MARILYN COE LAID the clutch on the sofa next to her. "We had an ongoing investigation of Chan and others, and I couldn't tell you about it at the time. When Riley Gunn got murdered, my boss was afraid you would come in and trample on everything we've set up."

"How long?"

"What?"

"How long have you been investigating Chan?"

"Couple of weeks."

Dalton felt his face heat up. "So I guess you already know a lot of what I've been snooping around trying to learn the last few days."

"Not necessarily. We were only interested in the drug connection."

"Yeah? I guess you didn't care that the drug connection might've played a part in the murders."

She gave him a pouting lip. "Well… I'm sorry, but we needed to nail Chan, and I couldn't bring you in on it. I asked, but the boss declined."

Dalton wondered if that was the truth, or if it was just her way of putting him off. "What do you know about Chan's hooks into Redgunn."

"We knew Hess was one of Chan's dealers and that he was a former roadie with Redgunn. We were watching him, but didn't have eyes on his place the night he got murdered. We assumed he was in bed by midnight and our guys left."

"So how did you know Colin Casey?"

"One night Hess strolled into the bar with him, so we decided to put the microscope on him, too. I got the job at the bar as a cover, because Hess was a regular there. I've tended bar before, and the owner hired me on the spot."

"I noticed he lets you come and go as you please."

"Yeah, I think he has a crush on me." Her tone sounded offhand, as if that happened pretty often. "Anyway, Hess and Casey came in again after I'd been there a few days, and I flirted a little with Casey. He asked me out to dinner one night and I went. I prodded him several times about drug availability, but he didn't let anything slip. Then the subject of the party came up, and he wanted me to go with him. I thought that was my chance to see inside the band and figure out who else might be involved."

"Were you successful?"

"No. But we're pretty sure somebody besides Hess was dealing, and maybe still is."

"Somebody in the band?"

"That's our suspicion. The best we can determine, it all began when they returned from Asia. Chan had been here for a while before that, but didn't show up on our radar until we arrested a dealer up in Marathon. He told us Chan killed his supplier and took over their territory. He said he's bringing in most of the cocaine in South Florida now. The guy we got tonight is just one of them. We suspect there's more, but we got lucky catching him since he's one of Chan's employees and was driving his vehicle."

It made sense that there was somebody else involved, and it could be Gunn and Hess's killer. Although Dalton had guessed Chan was pulling the strings, he thought it was only because of the lawsuit.

"You know Jack Ringo, the Key West PD detective?"

"I haven't met him," she said, "but I know he's investigating Hess's murder. Why do you ask about him?"

"I saw him coming out of Chan's suite at the Star Resort today. He lied about his reason for being at the resort when I told him I saw him. Said he was getting information about the place for someone who wanted to stay there. Chan wouldn't have anything to do with that."

"I'll ask my partner to check him out. You think he's in Chan's pocket?"

"That's my opinion, until I find out otherwise. Does he know about your investigation?"

"I don't think so. We suspected somebody with the police might be involved, so we didn't give them a heads-up. Your revelation about him meeting Chan makes me think that was a good decision." She stared for a moment, then said, "I never suspected you, though."

"I have a feeling you know a lot more you aren't telling me. You said Chan's drug business got off the ground after Redgunn returned from Asia. Do you know how that came about?"

"No, but we figured it wasn't a coincidence. Something must've happened over there. Maybe Hess linked up with them."

Nodding, he said, "Yes, something happened. Chan is part of a company called Eon Harbor, and Redgunn stayed at a hotel by that name in Thailand. According to one of the band members, Riley had some kind of episode with drugs and might have killed a woman."

Marilyn's eyes widened with a smile. "I knew it had to be something like that. Who told you about that?" She pulled her legs up underneath her. The gown rode up several more inches above the knee.

Dalton thought she was stringing him along, maybe playing him a little. "Like I said, one of the band members."

"So you're not going to tell me who?" She smiled. Her eyes were mesmerizing.

"It isn't important. Riley ended up in the hospital, and the band came straight home when he got released. I think the Eon people set him up so they would have leverage against him. At the time, his grandfather had a multimillion-dollar lawsuit against Chan's resort partner, Raven Gardner. The grandfather died sometime after that, but Riley went forward with the lawsuit. Later, he told his lawyer that the law firm representing Chan's company threatened him if he didn't drop it. It shook him up, and I believe the threat had something to do with what happened in Thailand." The words had just spilled out. He thought he should stop and get out of there.

"How about another drink?" she asked.

He glanced at his glass, which was empty, then to her smile. As attractive as this woman was, he had just learned that she had been lying to him. Granted, she was with law enforcement, but he still wasn't sure he trusted her. She was coming on a little too strong, and had practically admitted that her DEA mission was more important to her than stopping a murderer.

Someone knocked at the door. "Wonder who that is," Marilyn said, seemingly thinking out loud. She got up, eased over to the door, and peered through the peep hole. "It's my partner, Crandall Orr." Opening the door a crack, she said, "What is it, Crandall?"

Dalton heard mumbling, but couldn't put words with it.

"Okay," she said to her partner, "you didn't need to come by here. You could've called. Wait right there while I put on some clothes." She started to close the door, but stopped. More mumbling from outside. "No, you need to wait out there," she said and slammed the door.

She rolled her eyes as she passed Dalton. "Sorry, I have to go. They need my statement on the guy we arrested. Don't leave yet." She disappeared down the hall.

A couple of minutes later she returned fully clothed and Dalton stood from his chair. At the door, she wrapped her fingers around his wrist, pulled him close, and kissed him on the lips. As she lingered, Dalton realized his breathing had ceased and felt his heart thump in his chest.

When she pulled away, she said, "I was hoping you could stay. Maybe another time?" Without waiting for an answer, she opened the door and headed out. He followed, and Orr gave him the once-over. He was handsome, about Dalton's size, and looked as if he could handle himself in a fight.

"Who's he?" Orr said with a frown.

Marilyn locked the door. "None of your business. I'll follow you in my car."

"I could bring you back."

"No, that's okay."

The two agents drove away, and Dalton headed toward Little Torch Key and his cottage at his uncle's marina. A few minutes after turning onto US-1, he saw a car pull out behind him and follow. A fast food place came up on the right, and he turned in and got in line for the drive thru. The car behind him also turned in, but pulled over to the side. Dalton reached the window and asked for a cup of coffee. After receiving his order and paying, he pulled over and parked next to the car that had followed. A man got out, and Dalton realized it was Jack Ringo. He waited as Ringo stepped around to the open driver's window.

"Can I help you with something?" Dalton asked.

Ringo backed up a couple of feet. "Yeah, get out of the car." He had a tire iron in his hand.

Dalton took a sip of the coffee, which was surprisingly good for an evening purchase, and set the cup down. Ringo looked ready for a fight, and Dalton was willing to accommodate him. He exited the car keeping his eyes on the police detective's hands.

"You got a taillight out," Ringo said, his breath reeking of alcohol.

"Oh yeah?"

"Yeah, take a look." Ringo stepped to the rear of the vehicle and swung the tire iron at the taillight cover. It burst, scattering shards of red plastic on the pavement. "Looks like you've been involved in an accident."

"You're gonna pay for that," Dalton said, stepping over to the shattered light.

"Uh-oh, that sounds like a threat to me. You know something, partner? Throwing your weight around in Key West is a dangerous game."

"Yeah? How so?"

"I been a detective here for a lot of years, and you're a newcomer," he said, slurring his words. "I can make life real difficult for you, accusing me of something without proof."

"I haven't accused you of anything thing yet, but you're helping me make up my mind." He pulled out his phone.

"What are you doing?" Ringo slapped the phone from his hand. "You're not calling anybody. When I'm through with you, you'll head back to where you came from." The inebriated detective swung the tire iron, and Dalton lunged backward feeling wind from the make-shift weapon on his face. As Ringo completed the arc of his swing, Dalton kicked him in the stomach. He fell over backward, slamming against the concrete. He appeared stunned, but then roused and sat up.

"I guess that didn't work out like you planned," Dalton said. He picked up his phone, which was still in one piece.

"I'll see that you go to jail for that, assaulting a police officer," Ringo said.

"The security camera inside will show something different."

The downed man started to get up, and Dalton said. "Stay down. I won't be so easy on you the next time.

You probably haven't heard, but your friend William Chan is in hot water."

Ringo stared. "What are you talking about?"

"Chan's limo driver got busted a couple of hours ago smuggling in a cooler full of cocaine."

Something changed in Ringo's eyes. The hate drained away, replaced with what appeared as fear. "What does that have to do with me?"

"I saw you talking to him and Vici today, and you three looked pretty chummy. If you're involved in Chan's activities, you'll be going down, too." Dalton touched a couple of buttons on his phone and put it to his ear.

"Wait, who're calling?"

"Sheriff's office, to get you hauled in."

"No, no. Hear me out first."

"It's ringing, talk fast."

"Hang up, please. I'll fix the taillight. I promise."

Dalton closed the call and dropped the phone to his side. "Okay, I'm listening. Tell me about you and Chan."

Ringo struggled to his feet, leaving the tire iron on the ground. He looked beaten. "There is no me and Chan. I hardly know the guy."

Shaking his head, Dalton said, "Didn't look that way to me."

"Okay, so I went to see him. I admit that, but I don't have any business with him. You have to believe me."

"It's sounding pretty lame so far. Keep going."

"Vici called me a couple of times and asked me to do some things for Chan. They were nothing, and I knew Chan had a lot of juice, so I did what he asked."

"What things?"

"I fixed a ticket for his limo driver. Two times. He's a speeder, but I talked to the guy the second time and told him I wouldn't do it again. Then a few days ago, Vici said Chan needed information on somebody."

"Who?"

Ringo hesitated, then said, "He wanted details on you. I have a friend in administration with the state, and he sent me a copy of your personnel file."

Dalton didn't care what info they had on him, but it rankled him that somebody was that easily bought. "Okay, that's interesting, but it doesn't explain why you were in Chan's suite today."

"All right, I'm getting to that. Vici wanted the three of us to meet. He told me Chan wanted to hire me for his security team and the pay would be good."

"Let me guess: he said you could keep your job with the police department, too." Ringo opened his mouth but no words came out, which was as good as a *Yes*. "So, what's the first thing he wants you to do?"

"I didn't take the job. Told him I'd give him an answer tomorrow. Now I'm glad I didn't, if he's going to prison."

Dalton stared for a moment, not sure if he believed Ringo's story or not, but his explanation sounded more plausible than the one he'd given earlier in the day over the phone. "Get out of here. Replace that taillight first thing in the morning, or expect deputies to show up at your office."

Ringo nodded, picked up the tire iron, and headed for his car. He seemed a lot more sober than when he'd hit the pavement. When he drove away, Dalton went inside and asked for the security footage for the last few minutes. The night manager pulled it up. As expected, it captured the altercation. "Make a copy of that and send it to my phone." He gave the woman his number, and a few minutes later the video came in with a text.

THE NEXT MORNING, when he arrived at the office, Ringo waited in the parking lot. Dalton got out of the car and the detective said, "I got the part. I hope it fits."

"It better fit. I'll need that car in a little while."

At his desk he checked emails and found one from Randy Teal, the tech working on the locked phone. Teal said he couldn't get it open and asked if he should let the state lab give it a try.

Dalton stepped outside to the picnic tables, took a seat in the shade, and placed a call on his phone. As it rang, he watched Jack Ringo stand up and wipe sweat from his forehead. He had a screwdriver in his hand. When he saw Dalton, he stepped over and said, "You need to pop the trunk lid for me."

Sam Mackenzie answered the call and Dalton said, "Sam, it's Mick Dalton. Hold a second." He pulled his key fob and punched the button to open the trunk. When Ringo stepped out of earshot, he said to Sam, "Okay, I'm back. How's it going, buddy?"

"Doing okay, how about you?"

"Ah, problems, as usual. Goes with the job. I'd prefer diving for treasure. That was a good haul we made when you were down here."

"Yes it was. You need something?" Dalton had saved Sam's life a few months before, and he seemed happy to repay the favor whenever he had the opportunity.

"I hate to ask, after all the help you gave me in

Islamorada, but I have a locked phone that might be critical to a murder investigation. The techs with the sheriff's office are stumped, and I wondered if J.T. might take a look at it." J.T. a computer whiz, was Sam's friend, but he and Dalton had never hit it off very well.

"I'll give him a call. You know he has problems with law enforcement, so I won't promise anything."

After thanking him, Dalton hung up and headed to the entrance. As he passed the car, Ringo was still struggling with the repair. Inside, he went to Teal's desk and got the phone. If J.T. declined to help, he would try the DEA and see if they had any resources capable of unlocking the device. They might be interested in its contents, too.

As he reached his desk, Marilyn Coe called. "I apologize again about last night. Crandall could've handled the statement himself. He and the others did the takedown."

"No big deal. I got the impression he just wanted to see you."

"Yeah, he hits on me every chance he gets, and I'm not interested."

When she didn't add anything more, Dalton said, "You going to be able to tie Chan to the bust?"

"We think so. Crandall said they have him in for questioning, and his lawyer showed up right after he did. So far he hasn't said anything, but they're also working on the driver at the same time, and might get him to flip on Chan." After an awkward silence she said, "How's the murder investigation going?"

"Not so good. I have a few leads, but nothing that points to a particular suspect."

"I thought about your case after we left last night. Since we were targeting band members as potential dealers, we did workups on all of them. I can make them available if you think they would be beneficial to your case."

"Sure, that would be good. Did anything jump out at you?"

"You might find it interesting that Colin Casey had a different name before leaving Ireland. He was linked with a radical group accused of killing a public official in the U.K. Casey, who was known in his homeland as Aidan Reid, never got charged with anything, but he left right after that and came to the U.S."

TWELVE

THE FACT THAT Colin Casey was a member of a group accused of murdering a public official didn't automatically make him guilty. But entering the U.S. under an alias was suspicious. Marilyn, still on the phone, gave Dalton a link to the band members' background files. He read Casey's details first. Apparently, no one had ever gotten officially charged with the murder. It all happened about a year before Redgunn came into being.

"I don't see anything here on Aidan Reid, Casey's name in Ireland," Dalton said.

"We didn't look that far back. Interpol gave us information that isn't included in the file. They tracked him to the U.S., but I don't think they alerted immigration authorities. If they did, everybody must've forgot about him when he started a new life with the band. He was about twenty-five at the time and probably already had some musical experience to get Redgunn to take him on. He didn't appear to have any drug connections, and we dropped it."

"I cleared him early on," Dalton said, "because you were his alibi."

"Yeah, I was with him all night at his house when Riley got murdered. As I told you before, I slept on the sofa."

"Did you sleep the entire night?"

"I woke up once about seven in the morning and went to the bathroom. I heard Colin snoring down the hall. I had a hangover, and went right back to sleep."

"What time did you go to bed?"

"Must've been sometime around 3:30 or so."

"If you slept until seven, that gave him plenty of time to leave, do the murders and get back home." He thought for a moment, then said, "You think he could've slipped you a mickey?"

After a few seconds of silence, Dalton asked if she was still there.

"Yeah, I was just trying to piece it together. He was pretty wasted, and I told him I wasn't sleeping with him, so he insisted on us having a nightcap. I'd already had too much, but I agreed. It's a little fuzzy after that. I think he passed out in the chair, and I fell asleep on the sofa. The next thing I knew, it was 7:00 a.m."

"So, what're you saying?"

She sighed. "I don't think he gave me anything, but I guess it's possible. I had enough to drink to put me to sleep at three in the morning and to explain my hangover."

A tall man with tattoos, Casey could've killed Gunn and Hess, and could have assisted in killing Blake Owen. But why would he kill Gunn? That meant the end of the band. Casey seemed strapped for cash and was about to spend more on a new home. Why would he cut off the head of the golden goose?

"Thanks for the info," Dalton said. "I'll look over the rest of the files and see if any of it helps."

"You bet." She paused, then said, "I wouldn't turn down a drink or dinner sometime."

"Sounds good. I'll call you." When he hung up, he wished he'd said more. Such a beautiful woman, and there was plenty of chemistry, at least on his part, but he still wasn't too sure about her.

He perused the files on the other band members, but didn't learn anything new.

Crook stopped by and saw the phone inside the plastic bag. "That Hess's phone?"

"Yes."

"They find out what was on it?"

Dalton shook his head. "No, but I have a call in to somebody who might be able to crack it."

"It'll be too bad if it has evidence on our guy and we can't get it open."

"Yeah, it will. Say, let's go outside for a few minutes."

Crook gave him a questioning look, but said, "Yeah, okay. I could use a break."

Jack Ringo was gone when Dalton stepped out, and he walked around to the rear of his car to examine the taillight job. It looked like it did before Ringo shattered it. They took a picnic table in the shade of a cluster of palms, and Dalton told Crook about the DEA bust the night before and about Marilyn Coe working undercover at the bar. His partner whistled and said, "That's a shocker, but it probably doesn't help us any."

Dalton sighed. "No, but she gave me a link to some background they did on the band members that you might find interesting." He told him about Colin Casey, AKA Aidan Reid.

"Send me the link. I'll look it over and see what I can dig up on Reid."

"Sounds good. It might be a dead end, but you never know."

When Dalton got back to his desk, CSI Tarver called. "I have some plaster impressions of those shoe prints around the drainage ditch behind Blake Owen's property."

"Can you tell what kind of shoe it is?"

"There were two distinct prints. The larger one, a size eleven, is an athletic shoe, and I've narrowed it down to a brand. The other, a size seven, is probably a dress shoe, and it has a logo on the heel. It's an Italian make, and probably expensive. I checked, and two stores close to Key West carry them."

"Can you send photos and the information to my mobile?"

"Sure, I have your number."

The photos arrived a few minutes later and Dalton took a look. The larger one wouldn't be of any use unless he zeroed in on a suspect, but the smaller one might. He phoned Marilyn, thinking she probably hadn't gone in to work at the bar yet.

When she answered, he said, "Can you tell me where you're holding the guy you arrested last night?"

"Why do you want to know?"

"He's a suspect in the murder of Blake Owen, the man who planned to testify against the owners of the Star Resort."

"The limo driver is a suspect?"

"Yes. We have a witness that saw two men the night Owen was murdered. They were on the property that backs up to Owen's place, and they made shoe prints in the soft ground next to a drainage ditch that separates the properties. I have plaster impressions of the prints. One of them might be your guy."

"Okay, I'll have to clear it first. Give me a few minutes."

She hung up and called right back. "My boss said no dice, but if you send me photos our guys can see if they match his shoes."

He didn't like it, but thought that might be the best he could expect at the present. "How long do you think it'll take?"

"I'll ask them to do it right away."

"Okay, coming your way." He hung up and sent the image of the smaller shoe. An hour passed without an answer, and he called again.

"I forwarded the photo to Crandall," she said.

"This is really important. Your guy could be linked to my other murders, too."

"Okay, I get it." She sounded a little put off. "I'll check and see where they are."

When she called back, she said, "They didn't get a match. The size was the same, but he was wearing a boat shoe when they arrested him at the marina."

Dalton felt his hope leaking away. "He might own another pair that matches. Do you have a warrant to search his home?"

"They're working on that now, but he's William Chan's nephew and lives at his residence. It seems we're having difficulty getting a judge to sign off on it. Chan has a lot of juice around here."

"Is Chan in custody right now?"

"No. We had to cut him loose. They're still hoping the nephew will flip on him, though."

That didn't seem likely to Dalton. The guy wouldn't squeal on his uncle to save his own skin. "If you get a warrant, please have somebody look for the shoes."

"Okay. I have to go to work at the bar in a little while, but I'll let Crandall know."

"Oh, by the way, what's the nephew's name?"

"Charles Chan."

"Charlie Chan? You're serious?"

She chuckled. "Yes."

When they hung up, Dalton thought about the nephew, that he could be their only link to the three murders. He might not flip on his uncle, but he might give up another murder suspect if it meant avoiding the death penalty. The only problem was that the sheriff's office didn't have him in custody, and it appeared, at least for the present, that he was out of bounds for a sheriff's interrogation. With Chan's juice, the nephew could walk. If that happened, Dalton would be there to pick him up.

Dalton forwarded the information on the impressions to Crook, and then went by his desk. He told him that the DEA didn't get a match. "Can you check with the two stores Tarver cited and see if anyone there remembers him or his uncle buying the dress shoes?"

"Yeah, I guess so. I haven't found anything online on Aidan Reid. Maybe that's an alias, too."

"Yeah, could be."

Back at his desk, Dalton phoned the federal courthouse on Simonton Street. He asked for the clerk of the court, and it took a couple of transfers before getting him on the hook. After identifying himself, he asked if an arraignment was scheduled for Charles Chan.

"Hold on." The clerk sighed, as if he had better things to do than track down information for the sheriff's office. He came back a minute later. "Yes, Mr. Chan is due to see the judge at two today."

Dalton thanked him and glanced at the clock: a little past one. He phoned the watch commander and asked for a cruiser to be sent to the Federal courthouse by 2:00 p.m. to pick up Charles Chan for questioning. "I expect him to be released, and I want the deputies to grab him as he comes out the door."

The commander agreed and hung up.

He had missed breakfast and decided to get something to eat on the way to the courthouse. About halfway there, he turned into a restaurant and ordered a Cuban sandwich. It arrived with soft bread, fresh ham and pork, pickles, and a hint of mojo sauce and mustard. Very tasty.

When he finished eating and paid, he headed on to Simonton and parked on the street across from the courthouse. He stepped over to the sheriff's cruiser that sat a couple of spots away with the engine running. The driver lowered the window, and he leaned down and described Chan for the two deputies. "I expect him to make a run for it when he sees you. You probably should park over the curb in front of the building so you can grab him as soon as he comes out. I don't think security will bother you."

"Don't worry, we'll get him."

"Okay, just be alert."

The deputy, a man of about twenty-five, gave him a condescending smile.

As Dalton stood up, a black SUV eased by. The windows were tinted so dark he couldn't see inside. He leaned down again and nodded toward the vehicle. "I bet that's his ride. Probably imports from Miami inside it. If so, they'll be armed. Call and get another cruiser over here."

Not smiling anymore, the deputy nodded and got on the radio.

Dalton entered the building, flashed his badge for the security officers, and found the courtroom. He took a seat in the rear as Chan, accompanied by two marshals, shuffled in from a side door. Douglas Vici waited for him at the defense table. After the U.S. Attorney cited the charges, Vici argued that his client was innocent and that his misfortune was due to some bizarre mistake. Stating that his client was not a flight risk, he accepted personal responsibility for his appearance at trial. The judge contemplated only a minute or so before granting Chan's temporary release to the attorney. One of the marshals came over and ushered him out the door, probably to attach an electronic tracking device.

Dalton followed Vici as he made his way to the vestibule. Several people passed by, and he didn't think Vici saw him. He waited in the corner as the lawyer paced the other end of the large room. A few minutes passed, and then Charles Chan appeared through a side door, led by a marshal, who turned and went back inside. Vici and his client headed out the door, and Dalton went out behind them.

Two cruisers were on the curb, and two deputies stood next to the lead vehicle, both wearing vests. Two other deputies remained behind the wheels of the cars. Vici and Chan stopped when they saw what waited for them. The SUV sat idling on the street to the left. Another car sat at the curb about thirty feet behind the SUV.

One of the deputies stepped over and said, "Mr. Chan, we need to take you in for questioning in a murder investigation." Lawyer Vici had a look of surprise on his face.

Two Asian men exited the SUV and strode toward them carrying what appeared to be AK-47s. "Get in the truck," one of the men said to Chan in accented English. Then three men wearing DEA vests exited the car behind the SUV. Dalton recognized one of them as Crandall Orr, Marilyn's partner.

Several people exited the courthouse doors, saw guns, and hurried back inside.

Orr yelled at Chan, "They're going to kill you. Stay where you are."

One of the men with an AK turned and fired a burst at Crandall, who went down. One of the other DEA guys fired back and dropped the shooter. The other man with an AK shot a burst at Chan and then turned on the deputies. Before he could fire, Dalton put two bullets in his chest. The driver of the SUV sped off, screaming the tires on the pavement as he fled the scene in a haze of smoke. One of the deputies hurried over and collected the assault weapons. Both assassins lay in pools of blood and appeared dead.

"I've got this covered," Dalton said to the deputies. "Go after him."

They hurried to the cruisers and sped after the fleeing vehicle. Dalton called 911. He identified himself and said, "We need EMTs at the federal courthouse on

Simonton. Four men have been shot. One is a federal officer." After hanging up, he stepped over to Chan, whose dead eyes stared at the sky in horror.

Vici knelt by the downed man. "He's gone. No pulse."

Dalton hurried down the curb to Crandall Orr. One of the other agents was helping him up. He wore a protective vest, and blood streamed down his arm.

"You okay?" Dalton asked.

Orr gave him a frown. "No, the dude shot me."

"You're lucky to be alive. EMTs are on the way." As he said it, sirens droned in the distance.

The EMT truck arrived a minute later, and one of the medics went to work on Orr. Another headed over to Chan. After kneeling next to him, he said, "Nothing we can do for him."

Another sheriff's cruiser arrived, followed by two Key West PD squad cars. Dalton got them all together and described what had happened. The deputies and police officers worked together to take statements from Vici and the DEA agents.

Jack Ringo rolled up as Dalton readied to leave, and he had to repeat everything to him. "Your officers are getting all the details from the witnesses. I'll email you my official statement."

Ringo nodded. "That's fine." He paused, then said, "The taillight work okay?"

"Yeah, I didn't notice a problem with it." He headed to his car and drove away. Thinking about the news, he phoned Lola Ann. This would be a good one to toss to her, in case he needed her later.

"About time you called me. What's going on?" she asked.

"I have something for you, but it has to be from an anonymous source. You okay with that?"

"You got it cowboy. Fire away."

He described the courthouse scene in detail, including only Chan and Vici's names. "A DEA agent shot one of the assassins, and a sheriff's deputy shot the other." She thanked him and hung up. He assumed it would air within a few minutes.

Back at the office, he went in and briefed the lieutenant on what had happened, including the DEA bust the night before.

"Tell me again why you wanted to bring in this Charles Chan." Springer said.

"I believe he was one of the two men who killed Blake Owen, and he could've identified the other man. The other man probably also murdered Riley Gunn and Wilbur Hess."

"It sounds like you got him killed."

"That isn't the way I see it. The shooter killed him so he couldn't talk. His uncle might even have given the order. If not him, somebody more powerful. They probably would've waited until they left the courthouse if the DEA guys hadn't shown up. Either way, Charles Chan was a dead man."

Springer gave him a smirk. "Okay, you know the drill."

Nodding, Dalton pulled his service weapon and badge and laid them on his supervisor's desk.

"I expect a full report ASAP," Springer said. "The sheriff won't be happy."

Dalton left without commenting. He imagined the sheriff wouldn't like it any more than he did. Chan had been his only link to the other murderer. He sighed as he sat down at his desk.

Crook called and said he'd hit pay dirt. "I showed the driver's license photo to both stores and one of them said the younger Chan purchased the shoes just a couple of weeks ago. He remembered, because the shoes are expensive and no one else has bought any since that time."

"Okay, good work, Buddy. There was a shootout at the Federal Courthouse—"

"Yeah, I heard something about that on the news. You know what it was about?"

Dalton told him.

"Huh. Then I guess it doesn't matter if they were his shoes or not."

"Yeah, it matters. That nails him as one of Blake Owen's murderers. We just have to find the other one."

"Okay, I guess. I'm coming in."

A minute or so after they hung up, his phone chimed again and he answered.

"This is J.T. Sam said you have a problem with a phone."

"Yeah, thanks for calling. I have a phone that's locked, and the techs here can't open it. It belonged to a murder victim, and I believe it might have information on it that points to his killer."

"Sam told me all that. He said I probably couldn't open it either, and I bet him a hundred dollars I could."

Pretty smart of Sam to challenge him, otherwise, he probably would've never called. J.T. asked if the device had an IMEI number on the back. It did, and Dalton gave it to him.

"Okay, turn the phone on, and I'll call back when I get it unlocked."

He did as instructed. A few minutes after they hung up, he noticed Hess's phone light up, and pages of seemingly random text and characters streamed over its screen. Dalton set it aside and wrote up his report of the shooting. When he finished he sent a copy to his partner, the lieutenant, the sheriff, and Jack Ringo.

Crook came in later and dropped off the information he had gathered on the shoes. As he walked away to his desk, Dalton's phone chimed. He glanced at the display: J.T. again.

"Any luck?"

"Oh, yeah. Piece of cake. I looked at the content, and there's a video on it I think you'll want to see."

THIRTEEN

DALTON PICKED UP the phone and selected the camera function. There were no photos and only one video. He played it, and it began with blurring images, the picture moving erratically. It seemed that the person was getting into a vehicle, holding the camera down by his side. As the action settled, the lens peered upward at a passenger across from the camera. Dalton recognized the man: William Chan.

The video appeared to have been made in the rear of the elder Chan's limousine. Chan began speaking to someone across from him and to the left of the camera. "You said you want a piece of the action. Wilbur could be a rich man, but is unwilling to do what it takes." Chan nodded toward the person holding the camera without looking at him. "Riley is trying my patience. He thinks he can do business as usual and continue with this ludicrous lawsuit. He obviously does not know me very well. Kill him and I will give you his territory."

"Glad to." The words came from the person not in view.

"Do it tonight, and take Wilbur with you. Don't mess this up, or you'll be the next to go." Chan nodded toward the door. "Get out."

The images became erratic again, and then the video ended. Dalton glanced at the date and time the file was created. It was about nine hours before Riley Gunn was murdered. He leaned back in his chair and digested what had happened. It was apparent that Gunn was involved with the drug distribution along with Hess. Something Dalton hadn't considered.

Hess had attended the meeting in the limo, along with the person to whom Chan had spoken. From what Chan had said, Hess had been offered the job of killing Riley and had declined. He probably knew Chan planned to offer the deal to the other person and made the recording as insurance in case things went haywire.

While the video implicated Chan in Gunn's murder, it didn't identify the person he asked to do it. Dalton played it several times, trying to get a fix on the voice, but the man had said only two words, and he decided they could have been spoken by any number of males he had interviewed. He thought about the argument between Hess and Gunn outside Hess's home. He wondered if Hess had said something in anger about Chan planning to get rid of Gunn, maybe even flaunted the video. Gunn might have held the phone. He had gotten his prints on it somehow.

Dalton's first inclination was to arrest Chan and get a search warrant, but he needed his weapon and badge. He grabbed the phone and went by Crook's desk. "The phone is unlocked, and there's a video on it." He played it for him.

"Sounds like we've got him." He glanced at the clock. "You going to pick him up today?"

"I hope so. I'm going to see Springer. Come along if you want."

"That's okay. I need to wind up some things here."

He thought Crook probably wanted to head out to a gig. "Okay, that's fine. Just wanted to read you in."

When he got to Springer's door, the lieutenant said, "I just finished your report. You should be cleared pretty fast."

"That's good. I wanted to let you know that we got Wilbur Hess's phone unlocked and there's a video on it that shows William Chan ordering the hit on Riley Gunn."

The lieutenant gave him a wary look. "Let me see what you have."

He accessed the video and placed the phone on the desk in front of Springer. As it played, his eyes grew large. When it ended, Dalton said, "We need to arrest him, but he probably has some pretty high connections."

"Yeah, well, he isn't above the law," Springer said, sounding brave, but his wide, blinking eyes gave him away. "Maybe the sheriff needs to see this. He'll be the one getting the blowback." He picked up Hess's phone and they headed down the hall.

As they passed Sheriff Diaz's secretary, she said, "He's on a call," but Springer waved her comment away, and they stood at the doorway. Diaz looked up and narrowed his eyes. He said to the person on the other end, "I'll have to get back to you," and hung up. "This must be important. What's up?"

After viewing the video, he said to Springer, "Give Dalton his badge. I read his report. He shot a man trying to kill one of our deputies with an assault weapon. I'll take the heat if there's a problem." To Dalton: "Go get this guy. I don't care if he's the mayor's best golfing buddy."

When Dalton got back to his desk, he called Connie Duval in the Monroe County DA's office to give her a heads-up.

"Yeah, I know that guy," Duval said. "He spoke at a fund raiser for a local charity. You're sure of what you have?"

"I can send you a copy."

"Yes, do that."

Dalton sent it to her on the protected network and phoned the watch commander and told him what he needed.

"Okay, but I hope it doesn't turn out like the situation at the courthouse. By the way, deputies caught the driver. They cornered him in a shopping center. Our guys were worried he would come out spraying bullets. He sat in the vehicle for a long time with a phone to his ear, maybe calling for help. If that was the case, he must've struck out, because he finally exited with his hands up."

"That's good news. They take him to the jail?"

"Yes. What do you want us to do with him?"

"I'll send you my report from the courthouse shootings. Book him on felony murder, and I'll get by later. As for William Chan, I think taking him down will be peaceable, but you never know. I'm going to the Star Resort and ask him to come in for questioning. Maybe he'll agree if he doesn't know we're going to arrest him. You need to send a cruiser over there just in case."

"Roger that. It'll be there in twenty."

"Tell them to wait in the parking lot so he doesn't get suspicious."

As he stood to head out, Duval called back. "There

could be some problems, but the video looks pretty damning. Let me know when you have him in custody and I'll drive down."

"Will do."

He headed to the Star Resort and passed the sheriff's cruiser as he reached the parking lot. Continuing on, he turned toward the employee lot on the side and looked for the limo. It seemed to be missing, but the black Range Rover sat in its space. Apparently the DEA had released it back to Chan, maybe after deciding it was of little use since they had retrieved the chest full of drugs. Dalton drove back to the cruiser and got out.

"I'm going to ask Chan to come in for questioning," he said to the deputy at the wheel. "It'll be easy if he buys it. If he doesn't, I'll call you." They traded phone numbers. "In that case, we'll drag him out the front entrance. He'll hate that."

The deputy grinned. "I'd rather drag him out. I heard what happened at the courthouse. He was probably responsible for that."

"Okay, watch for a black Range Rover to exit the employee lot on the side. Follow him and make sure he goes to the detention center. If he doesn't, pull him over and put him in cuffs."

Dalton strode through the lobby and took the elevator to Chan's floor. When he exited, he headed to the office door and knocked. No one answered, and he knocked again. After a few seconds, an older Asian man opened up.

"Can I help you with something?"

Dalton identified himself. "Mr. Chan's nephew was

murdered earlier today, and I need him to come in for some questions that might help us find his killer."

The man paused, then opened the door for Dalton to enter.

Chan stood from behind his desk as Dalton approached. "What is this about?" he asked, his tone snappy.

"My condolences for your loss, Mr. Chan. I wanted to let you know that we caught one of the men responsible for your nephew's death. He's been uncooperative so far, and I need you to come in and see if you can identify him." A lie, but necessary.

Frowning, Chan said, "Why would I be able to identify this man?"

"We thought he might have been an associate of your nephew's."

Chan stared for a moment and then shook his head. "This has been so upsetting. I don't think I can do it."

Dalton sighed. "If you don't, we'll have to keep questioning the man until he breaks. That could take a while."

Something changed in his eyes, shifting from anger to what appeared to be concern. He probably wasn't certain the guy would hold up under pressure and wouldn't want him telling what really happened. "Very well. If you think it will help, I will come in."

"Good. He's being held at the detention center. I'll see you over there." He wrote the address on one of his cards and handed it to him.

When Dalton exited the elevator, he hurried out of the lobby to his car. Chan's SUV eased out the gate of the lot as he started his engine. The sheriff's cruiser waited a few seconds after Chan had passed, letting another car pull out behind him, and then followed. Dalton brought up the rear, hoping the deputies wouldn't get too close. They caravanned up N. Roosevelt in the fast lane and turned left onto A1A.

Chan's vehicle seemed to slow after that, and the other cars and the cruiser slowed as well. Dalton wondered if their suspect was trying to locate the turn onto College Road, or if he had spotted the deputies following. He passed the cruiser and the other car, and wedged in behind Chan's vehicle. No one was inside but Chan, and he was making hand gestures as if talking on the phone. As they neared the intersection at College Road, Chan's engine raced and he flew on through. He cut in front of a car and sped around another, his engine roaring.

So much for getting him to come in peaceably. Dalton floored his accelerator and tried to catch up, but there were vehicles between them blocking both lanes. He phoned the deputy and asked him to radio ahead.

Something had frightened Chan. Maybe his lawyer was on the phone and sensed that they wanted him for something other than to ID the man who had been arrested. Or maybe he spotted the deputies and smelled a rat. There was only one road out of the Keys, but there were other ways to escape, especially if you had unlimited resources. In Chan's case, he likely had suppliers with boats and aircraft. If he could separate himself from his chasers, which he seemed to be on his way toward accomplishing at the present, he might leave the Keys and never be found again.

A few miles past the Key West Naval Air Station,

Dalton lost sight of Chan's vehicle. He had seen two cruisers turn onto the highway ahead, running flashers, and could only hope they would catch up to their quarry. Weaving in and out of traffic, he saw a mob of flashing blue lights in the distance. It appeared they had turned off the road and were headed toward the coast. Dalton followed the last cruiser as it turned off to the right. They raced through a neighborhood, and up ahead he could see that they had stopped. He slammed on brakes and got out. Chan was running toward a boat idling in the water. If he made it, they would lose him. Then, as Chan reached the edge of the water, he motioned for the boat to come closer. One of the deputies caught up with him and tackled him to the ground. The boat sped off, full throttle.

Dalton hurried to the downed man and said to the deputy, "Cuff him and take him to the detention center. I'm going to follow you in and book him on a murder charge."

Chan's eyes darted to him, surprise on his face. "I haven't murdered anybody. You'll lose your job over this."

"Yeah? We'll see about that." On his way to the jail, he phoned Connie Duval and told her what had happened.

"I'm on my way. It'll take me about an hour to get there."

"That's fine. He'll lawyer up by then. I'll let you spring the video on him, if you want."

She chuckled. "It'll be my pleasure."

"I'm hoping it'll scare him enough that he'll give up the guy who pulled the trigger."

"Yeah, well, we'll turn the screws."

Upon booking the prisoner, Dalton drove over to the office and went in to brief the Lieutenant.

Springer was still at his desk and waved him in. "I heard you had a chase on your hands."

Dalton shrugged. "Yeah, a miscalculation on my part. I should've cuffed him at the resort and taken him out the front door."

"Well, you got him. That's the main thing, and his running just demonstrates his culpability. Work on him and get the shooter's name."

"Roger that." He headed to his desk thinking things could have gone worse with his supervisor.

Duval called a few minutes later saying she would arrive in ten minutes, so he headed back to the detention center. On the way, he called Marilyn and told her he had Chan under arrest. "We have hard evidence that he ordered a hit on Riley Gunn."

"Hard evidence sounds like you have a witness."

"Something like that."

She paused, then said, "Are you going to search his place?"

"Yes. I'll share anything we find concerning drug activity."

They hung up as he turned into the parking lot. Duval was exiting her vehicle and they walked together. At the door, Dalton stopped her and said, "What kind of deal can we make him if he gives up the shooter?"

"I've been thinking about that. We could give him twenty years instead of life without parole."

"Okay, let's see how that plays."

They went inside and found a room they could use

for the interview. Dalton asked one of the deputies to bring Chan in to join them. When he arrived, Douglas Vici trailed in behind him.

After introductions and starting a recording of the proceeding, Vici said, "I want to know what evidence you have on my client suggesting he had anything to do with a murder."

Duval said, "That's why we're here, Mr. Vici." She accessed the video on her phone and laid it on the table between the lawyer and his client. Both watched, their eyes wide.

When it ended, Vici glanced at Chan, then turned to Dalton and said, "Where did you get this?" His tone was thick with indignation.

Dalton shrugged. "We found it on a phone hidden in another murder victim's home, that of Wilbur Hess."

Chan scowled, leaned back in his chair and stared at Vici.

"You're going up for life with no parole," Dalton said. "If you give up the identity of the person you ordered to kill Gunn, Ms. Duval might cut you some slack."

Vici frowned. "How much slack?"

The prosecutor leaned back and waited a few beats, then said, "I can offer twenty years. He might get out sooner with good behavior."

Chan shook his head. "Twenty years? No way."

Sighing, Vici said, "I need to confer with my client."

"Sure, but don't take too long. The deal won't be available if we locate the shooter."

They stood to leave, and Vici said, "Please turn off your recorder."

Dalton did as asked and he and Duval went out.

After only five minutes, Vici stuck his head out the door and said they were ready. With the incriminating video, Dalton expected Chan to cave. Back inside the room, with the recorder running, Vici said, "My client has decided to take his chances in court."

WHEN DALTON GOT back to the office, he prepared an application and affidavit for a warrant to search William Chan's residence and his personal phone. With the information provided, he had no trouble securing a signature from a local judge, even given the late hour. He dropped by the jail and signed out Chan's phone and door key, and then headed to the man's home.

Inside, he went through it, room by room. When he located the office, he went to work on a home computer. He found no e-mails or social media accounts, but the browsing history indicated that he had visited an off-shore bank a number of times. It probably meant he had an account there. While that might be important to the DEA's case, it didn't seem high on Dalton's list for the murder investigation.

When he finished with the computer, he searched the desk and a file cabinet where he found lots of paperwork. Sifting through it turned up nothing connected to the murders, or even drug activity. Most of it related to the acquisition of the Star Resort.

In the master bedroom he went through items in the closet, a night table, and the connected bathroom, and didn't even find any prescription drugs. After an hour of searching the other rooms, he gave up and left.

Back at the office, Dalton caught technician Randy Teal about to leave after putting in overtime. He handed him the phone. "This belongs to a man named William Chan. He's been arrested for murder. Record the numbers of any calls and texts, and identify their owners if you can."

Teal agreed to look at it the next morning, and Dalton went on to his desk to document his search. He thought he might ask Crook to go back to the house with him the next day, if they didn't have much going on, and take another look. Chan had been meticulous in avoiding any records concerning his criminal activities. Dalton hoped the phone would provide more. Remembering that he hadn't examined anything other than the video on Hess's phone, he took it out and powered it up. He checked the call history, but didn't find any. No texts either. Apparently, it wasn't Hess's primary phone, which had never been found, and he had used it only to record the incriminating video. Dalton sighed and returned the phone to his desk.

THE NEXT MORNING Dalton locked up his cottage at 7:00 a.m. and went out on the deck where his Uncle Eric had prepared coffee and pastries for his guests. Eric did that several times a week, and everybody seemed to enjoy getting together for a freebie. Cupcake lay at his uncle's feet and stood when he saw Dalton coming. He went over and scratched the big cat's ears before grabbing coffee and a Danish. Three or four people sat around nursing their coffee.

"You making any headway on your investigation?" Eric asked.

"I have a couple of things that might pan out."

His uncle grinned. "I guess that means, 'No.'"

"Yeah, pretty close."

Eric turned to his guests. "He's investigating the Riley Gunn murder."

One of the guests, an older man nodded. "Yeah, I wondered how that was going, myself." Before he could say more, Dalton told his uncle, "Gotta get going. I have an early meeting." It was a lie, but he didn't want to get into a discussion. "Thanks for breakfast." He headed to his car and drove away, eating most of the pastry before getting to the end of the long, winding, driveway.

About ten miles down the road, his phone rang— Springer—and he answered it.

"I got a call a few minutes ago from the 911 center. When the guard at the jail made rounds this morning, he found William Chan dead in his cell."

FOURTEEN

WILLIAM CHAN LAY face up on the jailhouse bunk, his eyes closed and his arms by his sides. The guard, whose nametag read *Wallace*, opened the cell door, and Dalton and Crook entered. "That's the way I found him," Wallace said. "He looked like he was asleep, but he didn't wake up when I yelled at him to get up for breakfast."

"You have any idea how he might've died?"

Wallace shrugged. "I figure heart attack. He's what, maybe sixty?"

Dalton nodded. He didn't really know Chan's age but guessed the guard was about right. "You talk to any of the guys in the other cells about it to see if they heard him call to anybody for help?"

"No. I figured you would do that."

They went out, and Dalton asked him to relock the door. A man in the next cell over stood at the bars looking out.

"You hear anything next door during the night?" Dalton asked the man.

He narrowed his eyes, as if concentrating. "Something woke me up around midnight. Sounded like a cell door opening. I didn't hear it close again, so I must've gone back to sleep...or I could've just been dreaming the whole time. Why, what happened?"

"Nothing you need to worry about," Wallace said.

They asked to see the jailer and the guard took them to Alvin Banks' desk. "You need me for anything else?" Wallace asked.

"Not right now," Dalton said, "but I might have some questions later."

"Okay, I need to get busy on my rounds." The guard appeared relieved as he hurried away.

The two detectives introduced themselves to Banks. He shook his head. "Heck of a thing, huh?"

"Yeah, pretty curious," Dalton said. "The guy next door said he thought he heard Chan's cell door open around midnight. You have any video that would show that?"

"We should. Hold on a minute." He went to his security monitors and punched some keys on his computer. "You said around midnight?"

"Yes. Let's start around eleven and go forward."

Banks brought up the video and fast forwarded until a guard appeared around eleven-thirty. He slowed the footage to actual time and they watched the guard saunter down the corridor. "He's on rounds," Banks said. "He's passing William Chan's cell now." The guard kept going and disappeared around the corner farther down. Banks started fast forward again, and nobody appeared until 12:05 a.m., another guard going by Chan's cell, except this time he stopped and backed up. He opened the cell door, went inside, and stayed only a minute or so before coming out.

"Is it customary for a guard to enter a cell alone?" Crook asked.

Banks shook his head. "No, but maybe he thought the guy needed help."

Dalton nodded. "Who was the guard?"

"Let's see," Banks said, referring to a sheet on his desk. "That would be Otto Edwards. He comes on at midnight and works until eight. I didn't see him when I got here this morning, so he must've left early."

"He didn't tell anybody anything about Chan?"

"Hmm, I need to look over last night's report. I never got around to my email after making the 911 call." He brought up his messages and found one from the night jailer. "Nothing unusual happened," he said reading through it. "Except it Looks like Edwards didn't stay long after starting his shift. At 12:15 a.m. he sent a text to the jailer that he was sick and had to leave."

Alarm bells chimed in Dalton's head. "That was right after he went into Chan's cell. Are guards allowed to leave without seeing a supervisor?"

"No, I'll have to counsel him on that. Bob said he had to scramble to get somebody to take his shift."

"Run the video back to when he appeared in the corridor and play it again, slo-mo."

The jailer did as he asked. The guard in the footage had his back to the camera, and he wore a long-sleeved shirt and a cap with his uniform.

Dalton had a bad feeling. "Let's see the video of him arriving for work."

Banks stared for a moment, and then turned to a different monitor and brought up footage of the building entrance starting at 11:30. Three guards entered shortly before twelve. Once they had cleared the view, the man with the long sleeves and cap showed up at 12:03. He peered down as he used his card key on the lock, and his face was not visible under the brim of the cap. Upon entering, he stepped out of the camera's view. When he returned a few minutes later and exited, he again turned his face away from the camera. The other guards had worn short sleeves and no cap. Dalton asked Banks about that.

Banks shrugged. "It can get pretty chilly in here at night with the air blasting, and some guards wear long sleeves. The cap is optional, unless the brass is around, and then everyone wears it."

Dalton called Springer and asked him to send out the CSI team and the medical examiner.

Banks' eyes widened. "You think Chan was murdered?"

"Yes, that's what I think. I need Edwards's address." When the jailer gave it to him, he said, "Don't let anybody go inside that cell except the CSIs and the ME."

Dalton and Crook hurried out the door and drove to the residence of Otto Edwards. He lived in a mobile home only a mile or so from the jail. When they arrived, there were no vehicles present.

"Doesn't look like he's home," Crook said.

They got out and went up the steps to the front stoop. The door stood ajar. Dalton glanced at his partner and they drew their weapons. Easing the door open with the toe of his shoe, Dalton called out, "Monroe County Sheriff. Is anybody in here?" No answer. He tried again and got the same result.

The two detectives stretched on vinyl gloves and entered.

"I'll check the rooms down the hall," Crook said.

Dalton surveyed the small living room. It was dusty, but no clutter, and nothing appeared out of place. A large screen TV sat in the corner. The sofa looked as if no one ever sat on it, and there was a recliner, and a table next to the chair with a lamp and an ashtray. A couple of cigarette butts lay in the ashtray, the only indicator that someone lived in the place. The adjoining kitchen also looked neat and clean. No dishes in the sink, a trash container with three beer bottles in the bottom. The dinette table had nothing on its top, and a chair sat on either end of it.

"Come back here," Crook said from the hallway. Dalton headed that way. The bed had been made, but it looked as if someone had wrestled on top of it, the covers twisted and pulled down on one corner. Crook pointed to the wall on the far side of the bed near the closet. "There's blood spatter, down near the floor. I think it's still wet."

Dalton nodded. "Yeah, I see it. Smells like bleach in here."

Crook nodded. "Somebody cleaned up, but they missed that spot." He went into the connecting bathroom. "The shower curtain is gone, too."

A droplet of water hung on the showerhead from recent use, and the bottom of the tub was wet. A couple of shower hooks had smears of blood on them. Dalton pointed at the smears. "Looks like the person who took the curtain might've cut himself on one of the hooks."

Taking out his phone, Crook said, "I'll call Tarver and tell him to come here when they finish at the jail."

"How about staying here until the team shows up. I want to talk to the ME before he takes Chan's body away." Crook agreed, and Dalton headed back to the jail. Dr. Bragg was standing outside the cell as he came in.

"The jailer said you think this man was murdered," Bragg said.

"That's right. A man dressed in a guard's uniform entered the jail using Otto Edwards card key around midnight. He went directly to the cell and went inside, then left right after that. I'm pretty sure the guy wasn't Otto Edwards. Buddy and I went to his home. The door was open but he wasn't inside. There's blood in the bedroom and bathroom. I think the guy who came in here injured or killed Edwards and took his ID."

Bragg stretched on gloves and stepped inside the cell. "How do you think he was killed?"

"Probably drugs. Look for an injection site like you found on Blake Owen."

A few minutes later, Bragg said, "There's a puncture mark on his neck and bruising on his face. The perpetrator might've caught Chan while he slept and held his hand over his mouth while he injected him. I'll know if it was a drug that killed him after I test his blood."

As the CSIs finished up, Tarver told Dalton they had found several different fingerprints, but no blood. "The prints probably belong to guards and previous detainees."

Dalton hadn't thought about that; the killer could have been a previous detainee. When the prints came back, they could look into those other than the guards.

"By the way," Tarver added, "I sent you an email on the results from the Blake Owens house."

"Anything significant?"

"No. You already have the shoe impressions. The only prints we found were those of the victim. We didn't find any blood." That just meant that the killers were careful and wore gloves.

"Did Buddy Crook get in touch with you about Otto Edwards home?" Dalton asked.

"Yes, we'll be headed over there in a few minutes. He said there's blood."

"That's right. On shower hooks in the bathroom and on the wall."

Dalton left him to finish up and went to Bank's desk. "I want to see the video again of the guy entering the building."

Banks pulled it up on his monitor. After watching it again, Dalton said, "How could he have gotten in without anybody noticing he was an imposter?"

Shrugging, Banks said, "Well, he shouldn't have, but whoever was at the desk probably saw Edwards's ID and photo pop up on the computer when he used the card key and didn't think anything else about it. He could've gotten distracted with paperwork. I'm gonna have a talk with all my crew at shift change and warn them about staying alert."

"Well, I guess that's all you can do. How about looking up Edwards's auto information for me?"

"Oh, yeah, sure." The jailer seemed eager to move on from the subject of the breach. He searched a database and found that Edwards owned a white, late model Chevy Malibu. Dalton wrote it down, along with the plate number. "Bring up video from the parking lot around midnight when Edwards's car showed up."

Banks found the footage and started it up. "That's his car coming in now." Though midnight, the lot and the access road were well lighted. The Chevy entered the driveway behind two other cars. The driver parked in a space away from the other two. After the guards got out and entered the building, he followed a few minutes later. As with the other videos, the driver held his head down, and the bill of the cap obscured his face. Several minutes passed before the man returned to the car. He got back in and sat there for a few minutes, maybe sending the text to the supervisor about being sick. It was obvious that the killer wanted the jail to think he was Edwards, even after getting away, maybe to buy more time. Dalton wondered if Edwards's dead body was in the trunk and the killer needed get rid of it. "Can you back up and print a hard copy of the vehicle from the side and one that clearly shows the plate number?"

Banks did as he asked. Dalton phoned the watch commander and said, "I need an APB on a vehicle." He gave him the information and Edwards's address. "I think it was used to dispose of Edwards's dead body and might be pretty close to his home. Ask the deputies to start there and work their way out."

"You've been keeping my people pretty busy," the watch commander said.

"Yeah, I guess I have. You got something better for them to do than track down a murderer?"

"Well, since you put it that way."

After hanging up, Dalton drove out College Road and took a left on A1A, assuming the killer wouldn't go right into Key West to dispose of a body. He came to a tattoo parlor, turned in, and went inside. A man about sixty years old with scraggly gray hair tied in a ponytail sat behind the counter. His arms were nearly black with ink. Dalton showed him his badge. "You have security video for traffic out front?"

The man gave him a wary look. "Maybe. Why do you want to know?"

"Nothing to do with your business. I'm looking for a car that might've gone by this place last night around midnight."

The old guy shrugged. "Yeah, we got video."

"Can I see it?"

"The owner ain't here right now."

After waiting a few beats, Dalton said, "I can get a warrant and take your security system to the sheriff's office for analysis by our techs. Those guys find all kinds of stuff."

Tattoo Man stared for a moment. "Okay, I get your drift. Let's go to the back and I'll show you what we have." He sat down at a monitor and started up the video. The camera must have been mounted on the eave at the corner of the building, because it looked back toward the intersection of College Rd. Lighting was much dimmer than had been the case around the jail, but after a few minutes, the white Chevy came into view going north on A1A. Right after it passed by, another car followed.

"Run it back a minute or so," Dalton said.

The man did as he asked, and before the Chevy drove into view again, Dalton spotted the second car sitting alongside the road, as if waiting. As soon as the Chevy appeared, the second car pulled out behind it. An accomplice? If so, it would mean the killer could dispose of the car anywhere north of Key West and get a ride back to his car. Unfortunately, the license plate of the second vehicle was never visible, and the light was too dim to see a person inside either vehicle.

"Run it back again and freeze it on the car that just passed. I want you to print a hardcopy of it."

Tattoo man sighed, but did as he asked. Dalton left the place thinking the mystery car looked familiar, but that didn't mean much because it was a common style and color. He drove up the street to a service station and asked about looking at their security video. Upon viewing it, he learned that the Chevy and the mystery vehicle took a right on MacDonald Ave., which headed toward the Edwards address. That might have meant the killer was getting nervous and wanted to retrieve his own vehicle at Edward's home before somebody discovered it. If so, the Chevy could be close by.

The CSI team was already in place when he arrived. He parked on the street outside the mobile home behind a sheriff's cruiser. Inside, Crook said, "They bagged the shower hooks and swabbed the blood on the wall. They're dusting for prints now. After the deputies arrived, I told them to guard the place and I talked with the neighbors. Nobody said they saw anything. They're all working people who were asleep before midnight."

Dalton told him about the security videos and showed him the image of the mystery car. "I think the driver might've been his partner. The car waited alongside the road until the Chevy came out of College Rd. from the jail and turned north on A1A, and then it followed. Both cars turned on MacDonald and headed this way. So I think the Chevy might be close around here."

Crook said, "Huh, after Charles Chan died, he found somebody else to help with the dirty work."

"This person might've been helping all along."

"Well, I don't know how we can identify the owner of that vehicle. There must be hundreds of similar cars in the Keys."

Dalton nodded. "Yeah, it's too bad we don't have a plate number, but I think I've seen it somewhere since we've been investigating this case. I need to go back over my notes when we get back to the office."

Tarver came by and said they were finishing up and would be leaving in a few minutes. "Somebody cleaned the shower, but we sprayed luminal and found some blood spatter. That tells me the man was attacked in the shower."

"What about the blood on the wall?" Dalton asked. "You find any more there."

"Yes, some small spatter. It didn't appear to have been cleaned, so it probably was forgotten or went unnoticed."

"Sounds like there were two attacks: one in the shower and one in the bedroom."

Tarver nodded. "Yes, that's my conclusion, too. I'll try to send you my report later today."

"Okay," Dalton said. "I'm gonna take a drive and look for this guy's vehicle."

Crook said he would go along with him and they left. The neighborhood was a mixture of mobile homes and small houses. It was laid out in a rectangular grid that bordered a canal on the south end. They drove at a snail's pace down the street until it ended, and then took the next street below it going back the other way. There were few places where the car could be hidden since the lots were small and most residents parked in front of their homes or in small carports. As they neared the canal, Dalton wondered if he might have guessed wrong. He knew the Chevy had come in that direction, but could have gone on beyond Edwards's neighborhood.

At the end of the street next to the canal, they started back up the grid, retracing their search. At the third street from the canal, Crook said, "Back up. I think I saw something." Dalton put the car in reverse and eased it back until Crook told him to stop. The house appeared vacant. Weeds stood a foot tall behind a fence that surrounded the front yard, and a For Sale sign lay on the ground next to the street. A vehicle was backed into a thicket of palmetto next to the house. Only the grill and a white front bumper were visible. They pushed through the foliage to the rear of the car and found Edwards's license plate attached.

The driver's door was unlocked, so Dalton stretched on vinyl gloves, opened it, and popped the trunk lid. As he pulled out of the vehicle, Crook said, "Call 911. Edwards is back here, and he's alive."

FIFTEEN

EMTs ARRIVED WITHIN a few minutes. They pulled Otto Edwards's naked and unconscious body from the car's trunk and strapped it onto a gurney. Dalton peered into the open trunk. The shower curtain lay there in a wad. Blood spatter and droplets of water glistened on its surface.

A couple of deputies had shown up with the rescue team, and Dalton asked them to follow the victim to the ER and stand guard. When they hurried off, he called Tarver and told him the situation.

"I'll send somebody to look the car over. You think the guy's going to live?"

"I hope so. EMTs are loading him into the truck now. He took a blow to the side of his head. Drugs could be a factor, too. The ER should be able to tell us more, but it might be a while." Crook pushed through the brush and stared into the trunk. "Looks like Tarver was right about him being attacked in the shower."

"Yes, it does," Dalton said. "That means the blood on the hooks might belong to Edwards." He wondered if his disappointment showed in his face.

"There's still the blood on the wall. Maybe it belongs to the attacker."

Dalton nodded. "Yeah, maybe. It could also be more

of the victim's blood. Let's hope he survives so he can tell us what happened and ID the guy."

They waited around until one of Tarver's CSI crew arrived and had scanned over the vehicle. He told them he would have it towed to the county lot so they could give it a good examination. When the tow truck came and hooked it up, Dalton and Crook left and headed to the ER.

They found the doctor who had attended Edwards's wounds and asked about his condition. "He's still unconscious," the doctor said. "The head wound doesn't appear very serious, and probably not what's keeping him under. I'm thinking he's been drugged, so we're testing his blood."

Dalton gave him one of his cards and asked him to call when Edwards regained consciousness. He and Crook headed toward the office and got a sandwich on the way to eat at their desks. Before starting on the reports, Dalton checked email and ate his sandwich. Tarver's message concerning the Blake Owen crime scene didn't indicate anything beyond what he'd told him earlier: no blood, only the victim's fingerprints.

He started a William Chan murder file and documented what had happened at the jail and at the Edwards residence. As he finished up, Tarver called and told him they'd found some minute blood spatter on the bedspread. "I'm guessing it's the same as that on the wall, but we won't know for sure if it's different from that of the victim until we get DNA results."

"Can you put a priority on it?"

"I'll ask, and we can speed it up by hand-delivering it to the lab."

The killer had evaded the law after committing four murders and attempting to murder a jail guard. He had left no fingerprints or other evidence that could identify him. Dalton thought he might have gotten careless with Edwards, and was hopeful the blood would help identify him.

If it was the perpetrator's blood, unless he had committed a felony and his DNA was on file, they would still have to compare it against samples from suspects. They could sample everyone's DNA who had attended the party. That would be a good start, but maybe they could narrow it down first. He pulled out the Riley Gunn file and went over the names of people they had interviewed.

While still at the crime scene, he had spoken with Ana Kovich, the housekeeper. She seemed genuinely distraught over her boss's death, and Dalton hadn't thought any more about her. Crook found that she had overstayed her visa, but that didn't make her a murderer.

Colin Casey, the first party attendee to be interviewed, had an alibi with Marilyn Coe. She had left the party with him and slept at his home the rest of the night. After revealing that she was an agent with the DEA, she had told Dalton that Casey had a suspicious history with a radical group in Ireland, and had fled to the US after a murder in the UK. He had a good motive for murdering Gunn; he was over-extended and needed money. Gunn's insurance policy would net him $1 million. Gunn's safe may have contained a lot of cash. The video from Hess's phone showed William Chan offering the killer a potentially lucrative drug distribution territory.

As far as Dalton was concerned, Casey was at the top of the list, even though Marilyn Coe had provided him an alibi. Dalton believed her, but thought she could be mistaken, since she had slept in a different room. They needed a DNA swab from him.

Buddy had interviewed Alan Sheffield and his party date. They alibied each other, and Dalton and Buddy talked with them two more times. Sheffield seemed a little slippery, and seemed to be less than forthcoming when asked about Eon Harbor. He and his date had been drinking heavily the night of the party, and were also inebriated the first two times detectives had spoken with them. He had a motive for killing Gunn, too; he wanted more prominence in the band, and Riley held him back. Maybe he thought he could become the face of Redgunn if Riley wasn't in the picture. Though not at the top of the list, they needed a swab from him, too.

Dalton had spoken with Gunn's lawyer, Hilda Wright. She was far down the list of potential suspects, because it had been established that the killer was a tall person and probably a man. Both Dalton and Buddy interviewed the brothers from Canada. They wanted to produce a record for the band and seemed to have nothing to gain, and a lot to lose, by killing Gunn.

Though Jimmy Earl had not attended the party, Dalton had spoken with him at length at his home and in the sheriff's office. He didn't have a solid alibi, but Dalton was pretty sure he didn't kill Gunn. His vintage Camaro had been left in a vacant lot near the murder scene with the victim's blood inside, as if it had broken down. That looked bad for Earl, but there was a problem: someone had intentionally disabled the car, and that smelled like an attempted frame.

While not considered a suspect, Jack Ringo had admitted to doing favors for William Chan, and even considered a position to head up Chan's security. Dalton suspected the position required Ringo to maintain his status as a police detective. So, that didn't make him a killer, but would cause him a lot of grief if known by higher-ups. He would like to get a swab from him, too, but would need more evidence before opening that can of worms.

When he came to the video disks, Dalton inserted the first one into his computer. It was the one from the company that managed Riley Gunn's security system. It started up and showed all the party attendees arriving and one car leaving. A tingle ran down the nape of his neck. He backed the footage up to where the housekeeper, Ana Kovich, had driven off, and froze the image of her vehicle. It looked a lot like the mystery car that had followed Edwards's Chevy away from the jail. The camera on Gunn's garage had captured a better view from the side of the vehicle as it exited the garage and drove away. He froze the image and printed it.

Crook stopped by. "You finish your reports?"

"Yeah, let me show you something." He laid the printed sheet next to the one he had gotten from the tattoo parlor footage of the mystery car.

"That looks like the car. Who owns it?"

"Ana Kovich, Riley Gunn's housekeeper. Let's go check it out."

She lived in a duplex two blocks off the Overseas Highway on Big Coppitt Key. One side of the building had a For Rent sign on it. The housekeeper's car sat out front. As the two detectives climbed the steps to the porch, the door swung open. Kovich stood there, a look of shock on her face, holding the handle of a rolling suitcase.

"Looks like you're going somewhere," Dalton said.

"Yes, I don't have much time."

"We need to talk before you go."

"I told you; I don't have time."

"You mind if we look inside your luggage?"

"No, you cannot. I have my rights." She seemed like a different person from the meek woman who had cried as she spoke on the morning of Riley Gunn's murder. Dalton pulled out his phone and called the watch commander. He asked him to send deputies to pick her up for questioning. When he got off the phone, she said, "I have to go home for an emergency."

"What kind of emergency?"

"My mother is sick. She lives in Ukraine."

"We need to ask you some questions before you go. You need to bring your suitcase. When we finish, we'll take you to the airport, and maybe you can still make your flight." Dalton didn't want anything to happen to the luggage before they got a search warrant.

She remained silent, a frown on her face, as a sheriff's cruiser rolled up behind Crook's car. A deputy got out and ushered Kovich and her luggage into the back seat. Dalton and Crook followed them as they drove away. When they reached the office, Dalton told the deputy to lock her in an interrogation room. "Turn on the video in case she calls anybody." They prepared a search warrant for her home, luggage, automobile, and phone, and drove to the courthouse to find a judge.

An hour and ten minutes later, they returned and watched the video of her in the room. She stood a couple of times and tried the door knob, then knocked, but went back to her seat. Later she pulled out her phone, as if to call someone, but then turned it off and laid it down. Several minutes passed, and then she did the same thing again. This time she appeared to punch in a number, but before putting it to her ear, she turned it off. Other than fidgeting in her seat, there was no other activity.

They headed into the room and she jumped up from her chair. "You were gone so long. I need to leave right now to catch my plane."

"Sit down," Dalton said. "This'll only take a few minutes." He laid the printed automobile images from the tattoo parlor in front of her on the table.

"This picture of your car was shot early this morning. You were trailing this other car, which was stolen. The driver had just killed William Chan inside the jail. You followed him so you could give him a ride after he ditched the stolen car."

Tears streamed down her face. "No, I did not."

"Tell us who drove the other car. Things will go a lot better for you if you give him up."

"But I don't know what you mean."

"We can charge you with felony murder. You don't have to kill anybody for that; you just have to be along with someone who did. Felony murder carries a death penalty in Florida."

Her eyes grew wide as she wiped tears. "I want a lawyer. I know my rights."

"Sure. You have somebody in mind?"

"Yes. Mr. Douglas Vici." No surprise there.

They waited while she called him. "He wants to speak to you," she said to Dalton and handed him the phone.

"You can't question her until I get there," Vici said.

"You better get here in the next fifteen minutes, or your client will be headed to jail."

When they hung up, Dalton laid the search warrant in front of her. "This is for your home, car, luggage, and phone." After stretching on gloves, he picked up the suitcase, laid it on the table, and opened it up.

"My lawyer is coming. You can't do that."

"Sure I can."

The only thing he saw inside was clothing, but he lifted the items and found stacks of cash underneath. A quick count totaled to $300 thousand. A couple of the stacks had smudges of blood on them. There didn't appear to be any visible fingerprints in the blood, so he suspected the person handling it had worn gloves.

He wondered about her part in the plan. Did she open Riley's safe for the killer? It would make sense that she could figure out the combination, having been there day in and day out. She could have watched her employer enter the code, or he could've written it down and she found it. Dalton held up one of the bound stacks for her to see the blood. She gasped, as if seeing it for the first time.

There was also a man's Rolex watch in the bottom. It was in mint condition, and he knew it would be worth at least $30 thousand. Also in the bottom of the case were two pairs of gold cuff links and a man's ring set with a diamond the size of a macadamia nut. All in all, a large fortune for a thieving housekeeper.

The items probably wouldn't make it through customs at the airport. Her expired visa would likely be a problem too, but Dalton didn't think she intended to fly to Ukraine. She probably just wanted to get out of town. He did wonder why she had waited, though, and if she and the killer had intended to meet somewhere.

A deputy opened the door and ushered Douglas Vici into the room. "What are you doing? You can't go through her things."

Crook handed him the warrant. He frowned as he read it while standing, and then dropped it on the table. "I need to speak with my client. In private."

"Okay," Dalton said. "Follow me." Crook remained with the suitcase while he took them to another room. He asked a deputy to bring them back when they were ready.

The lawyer and his client returned a few minutes later and took a seat. "Ms. Kovich said you accused her of abetting a murderer," Vici said. "Please describe what you think she has done."

Dalton walked him through what had happened at the jail, and showed him the printed images of the vehicles. Vici gave him a smarmy smile. "Before I respond to your accusations, I'll tell you right now that I plan to sue the county over William Chan's death."

"I don't think so," Dalton said. "Once we catch the man who committed the murder, I suspect you'll be defending him. You can't do both."

Vici's face reddened. He stared for a moment, then said, "As for your accusations, that picture doesn't prove anything. There are many cars like it on the road. She said she didn't do it, and you don't have any proof that she did. You need to release her immediately."

"I want to show you something." Dalton picked up one of the stacks of cash that had the bloody smudge. "I believe this is Riley Gunn's blood. She wouldn't have this money if she wasn't involved in his murder. She also has a number of personal items that I believe belonged to him. Mr. Gunn's fingerprints will likely be found on them. I think she knew the combination to his safe and gave it to the killer. The items in that case probably represent her split."

The lawyer just sat there, a steeled expression on his face.

"I need to see your phone," Dalton said to Kovich.

She turned to her lawyer, a questioning look on her face. He nodded, so she took it from her purse and slid it across the table. Dalton turned it on and checked the call history. There were incoming and outgoing calls to several different numbers over the past week. One number repeated several times, and a call was made to it at 8:30 p.m. the evening Riley Gunn was murdered. The conversation lasted less than a minute, and Dalton wondered if she was talking with the killer, maybe to tell him the safe was open, or to give him the combination.

Dalton held the phone up to Kovich. "Who did you talk with at this number?"

She frowned and leaned forward, as if to get a better look. "It was a friend. I had some car trouble, and he said he would fix it."

Handing the phone to Crook, Dalton asked him to document the calls and numbers for the past week. He looked back at Kovich. "The DA might cut you a deal if you tell us the name of the killer."

Vici shook his head. "Ms. Kovich doesn't know anything about any murders. She told me that Mr. Gunn gave her the things you found in the suitcase."

"You're serious? That's your defense? He gave her a fortune in cash and personal items?"

"Yes, he gave them to her. She said he used drugs and was very generous when he got high. All you have is circumstantial evidence. It won't hold up in court. I suggest you release Ms. Kovich and save yourself a lot of disappointment."

Crook finished with the phone and Dalton gave it back to Kovich. He knew a slick lawyer like Vici could be convincing in court, and she might go free. Though pretty certain she had abetted the killer, he thought arresting her might not be the way to go at the present. "All right, she's free to go for now. We're closing in on the murderer, though, and if she doesn't give him up before we bring him in, there won't be any deals."

Vici gave him a smug smile. "She can't give you information she doesn't have." Turning to his client he said, "Let's go. I'll take you home." He stood and reached for the suitcase.

Dalton shook his head. "The suitcase stays here until we examine the blood."

The lawyer opened his mouth, perhaps to argue, but then seemed to think better of it. He and Ana Kovich headed for the door.

Dalton said, "Be careful, Ms. Kovich. Two people who could've named the killer have died within the span of two days. But I suppose if you really don't know who he is, you should be okay."

The former housekeeper's eyes widened, as if she hadn't thought that far ahead. He guessed that her case contained everything she owned of any value, and without cash to leave town, she would be a sitting duck. She turned and hurried out the door ahead of Vici.

"I'll usher them out," Crook said to Dalton.

Before he got out the door, Dalton went over and said, "How about taking the warrant and go ahead and give her home and car the once-over." Crook agreed, and Dalton asked a deputy to step in while he called Tarver to send someone over and inventory the suitcase.

Dalton had hoped Kovich would squeal, but he wasn't surprised. Since her visa had expired, he made a mental note to check with ICE and see if they would be interested in her case. A threat of deportment might give her a change of heart, and it might even save her life.

A member of Tarver's team came in and went over the contents of the case. She counted the cash, documented the presence of the other items, and took photos. Dalton watched, and he and the deputy signed off as witnesses before she took the case with her. On his way to his desk, his phone rang. Caller ID indicated it was the hospital, and when he answered a nurse told him Otto Edwards had regained consciousness.

He drove to the hospital and found Edwards in a recovery room inside the ER. The deputies stood directly outside with cups of coffee. He asked one of them to get the doctor for him. Inside, Edwards was awake.

The detective introduced himself. "We found you

in the trunk of your vehicle. Can you tell me what happened?"

"A guy slugged me while I was in the shower." He stared out the open doorway at nurses and doctors who passed by, his eyelids droopy.

"Do you remember anything else?"

"I think I was out for a while, but then I woke up wondering where I was and pulled myself out of the tub. I stumbled into the bedroom. The guy had his back to me, putting on the uniform I had laid out on the bed. When he turned around, I hit him. It connected, because I saw a string of blood fly from his nose." He lifted his right hand, formed a fist, and inspected his knuckles. They didn't appear to be cut, but one of them looked swollen and had dried blood on it.

Dalton called Tarver and asked him to send someone over to swab blood from Edward's hands. As he hung up, the ER doctor came to the doorway and motioned for Dalton to come outside.

They exited the room, and the doctor said, "His blood contained a high concentration of a narcotic. He could easily have died from it. As I told you in the ER, the head wound was not serious, and I think he'll be fine in a day or two. We'll let you know if there's any change. I have to get back." He turned and hurried away.

Back in the room Dalton said, "The doc told me you're going to be okay. Let's get back to what happened when you slugged the guy."

"He must've hit me again, because the next thing I know, I'm on the floor and he's sticking a needle in my arm. Everything is a blank after that, until a few minutes ago when I woke up."

"Did you get a good look at him?"

"I know he was big, about my size, and had dark hair. It must've been long, because it was gathered on top like a man bun." He stared out the door again, and his eyelids drooped, as if he might dose off.

"Anything else you can tell me about him?" Dalton asked. "I think this is the same guy who murdered at least four people, and you're lucky he didn't get you, too."

That seemed to wake him up. His eyes narrowed. "I've been trying to remember. There was something familiar about his face, like I might've seen him somewhere."

"He used your ID card to get inside the jail and murder a detainee. Knowledge of the layout at the facility would have helped him do that. You think he could've been a past detainee at the jail?"

"Maybe. There've been so many, it's hard to say." His last words were slurred. A few seconds later his eyes eased shut and he began snoring.

Dalton waited for the CSI to arrive and swab the blood sample from Edwards's hand. As he left the room, he told the two deputies to be alert for anyone going into the room. "Once the guy who put him here knows he's alive, he might come back to finish the job."

"Don't worry," one of the deputies said, "we've got it covered."

On his way back to the office, he called Crook, who was parked down the street from Kovich's residence. He said, "I didn't find anything significant in the house or the car. The lawyer stayed until I was finished, and he left when I did. I thought I'd watch the place for a while, in case somebody came by for a visit."

"Why don't you get some deputies to do that and have them alert us if anybody shows up."

"Roger that. I'll see you back at the office. Oh, yeah, while I was waiting, I called Randy Teal, the technician, and asked him to research that number from the housekeeper's phone."

"Good. Maybe it'll lead somewhere."

When Dalton got back to his desk, he searched for a database of detainees at the jail. It took a few minutes, but he found it, and sorted the names by date. He went back three months and scanned the names each day going forward. There were more than he expected. Most were charged with public drunkenness, disturbing the peace, brawling, or domestic violence, and a small percentage were in for more serious crimes. When Crook returned, he told him what he was doing and asked him to check the previous three months.

The going was slow. He had gone through about half the names an hour later, and hadn't recognized any of them. His desk phone rang, and he answered.

"Is this Michael Dalton, the detective?"

"Yes, can I help you?"

"This is Bobby Carson. You were over at my house a couple of days ago, talking about the two men that murdered that man around the block."

The retired autoworker with the flamingos in the yard. "Yes, Mr. Carson, I remember. What can I do for you?"

"I told you the big fella had a tattoo, and I think I know what it was."

"Yeah?"

"Yeah, I bought a magazine with pictures of tattoos, and I'm pretty sure the one on that guy was a Celtic cross. I'm looking at it right now, and I think it's the same one."

Dalton told him he would drop by and take a look at the picture. They hung up, and he wondered if the old guy really knew what he had seen that night. He searched for Celtic cross tattoos on the computer and lots of them popped up, but there was a similarity in all the images: each had a circle surrounding the intersection of the cross pieces. It appeared to be a common tattoo.

Crook hurried over to his desk. "Hey, a bunch of guys got locked up about five months ago for participating in a bar fight. Two of the names jumped out at me: Jimmy Earl and Colin Casey."

SIXTEEN

DALTON PRINTED PHOTOS of Earl, Casey, and the three other men who had been jailed for the brawl. He and Crook headed to the hospital. Edwards had been transferred to a private room.

"Everything okay?" Dalton asked one of the deputies outside the room.

The deputy nodded. "Quiet as a mouse."

The two detectives went in and found Edwards sitting up in bed, flipping channels on the TV with the remote.

"You must be feeling better," Dalton said.

Edwards glanced at him. "Yeah, lots better. The nurse said I could go home if the doctor approves it."

Dalton introduced Crook, then said, "We have some photos of men who were guests at the jail a few months ago. How about taking a look and see if you recognize any of them?"

"Sure, let's see them."

Crook laid the photos side by side on the tray table and wheeled it over the bed. Earl and Casey were last in the lineup.

Edwards picked up the first photo and narrowed his eyes as he studied it. He laid it down and got the second one. When he got to the last two, he laid them aside together. "These two look familiar."

"Does one of them look like the guy who slugged you?" Dalton asked.

Shaking his head, Edwards said, "Huh, I don't know." He pointed at the picture of Casey. "The hair color and length were similar to this one. But I only got a glimpse of the guy's face. I don't know if either of these was the guy, but both of them look familiar."

This hadn't gone as well as Dalton thought it would. Two of the other men had longish, dark hair, and he hadn't fingered either of them. "Look at all of them again."

Edwards shrugged and picked up the photos one at a time and studied them. "Sorry, I can't say." Then something changed in his eyes, and he grabbed up the same two shots. "Oh, yeah! I remember now. One of the other guards said these two were in a famous band."

It wasn't the kind of recognition Dalton had hoped for. He sighed.

"You think either one of them was your attacker?"

"Can't really say for sure, but I don't think so."

"Okay. I appreciate your taking the time to look."

They left, and in the car, Crook said, "What do you think?"

"I don't know what to think. I thought we had him. We still need the DNA." He pointed the car in the direction of Casey's home.

When they arrived, Crook knocked on the door. No answer. He tried again and got the same result. "His vehicle is here," Crook said. "Maybe he's around back."

Pushing through shrubs, they rounded the small house to the back yard. A rock song played from speakers on the apron of a swimming pool. Colin Casey lay on a lounger, a beer in his hand. His long hair hung in wet tangles. Dalton noticed his tattoos for the first time. A Celtic cross occupied a space of about four inches midway between the back of his hand and his elbow. He sat up, seemingly alarmed when they first came into view, and then a frown crawled onto his features. "What, you just invite yourself into a person's private space?"

"We knocked on the door," Dalton said, "and didn't get an answer. We need to talk to you about Ana Kovich."

He seemed to think for a minute. "You mean Riley's housekeeper?"

"That's right. How well do you know her?"

"Not very well. She's a looker. I asked her out once, but she said she was seeing somebody. What about her?"

"We just caught her trying to leave town with a suitcase full of money and valuables that belonged to Riley Gunn. She said they were gifts, but I don't believe it."

"No, he was too stingy." He raised an eyebrow. "You think she's the one who murdered him?"

"Maybe, but we need to ask you some questions, too."

"I had an alibi, remember? I thought you checked it out."

Dalton nodded. "I did, but Marilyn Coe said she slept in a different room, and couldn't swear that you stayed put all night."

"Well, I did. I was trashed. I couldn't have driven anywhere."

"Whoever killed Riley also killed William Chan at the county jail this morning."

"Who?"

"William Chan. Are you pretending you don't know him?"

"Yeah, because I *don't* know him," Casey said, his voice rising in volume with each word.

"Mind if we go inside?"

"Yeah, that's fine." He stood with his beer and grabbed a towel from the back of the lounge chair. They entered the back door, which went directly into the living room. Casey said he wanted to put on some clothes and headed down the hall. They took a seat, and Dalton pulled out his phone and punched in the number Ana Kovich had called. The house was small, and he hoped to hear a ringtone, but all he heard was the hum of the refrigerator a few feet away. Then someone picked up on the other end, but remained silent. Dalton held on for a few seconds before hanging up. He said to Crook, "If it's his phone, he must have the ringer turned off."

Casey returned a minute later wearing pants and a shirt. "Now, who's this Chan dude you mentioned?"

"William Chan was the head of the Eon Harbor group in Key West. He was also a local drug kingpin, and he was murdered this morning, probably so he couldn't name Riley Gunn's murderer."

"You're saying Chan knew who killed Riley?"

"That's right. We have a video of him ordering a man to kill him so he could take over Gunn's drug territory."

The Irishman's eyes widened. "Who else was in the video?"

"From what we could see, a guy who looked a lot like you."

"Are you kidding? No. It wasn't me." He took a nervous slug from his beer bottle and set it down. "Like I said, I didn't even know Chan."

"You knew Riley was distributing, though, didn't you?"

Casey sighed. "Yeah, I knew. It wasn't a surprise. He told everybody the band would have a comeback, but after Thailand, he didn't seem to care anymore. I think he just gave up after the drug money came rolling in. He said once that he never had to touch the product. So I guess that made it all right in his eyes."

"And that left the rest of you out in the cold." Before Casey could argue, Dalton said, "Chan's killer attacked a jail guard at his home and took his ID and uniform. He used them to get to Chan while he was in a jail cell, but he got careless and left some blood at the guard's home. We need a DNA swab from you."

"DNA?" Casey seem to think about that for a moment, then shook his head. "No, man. I didn't have anything to do with any of that."

"We can get a warrant, if you want to go that route. In that case, we'll include a search of your house and vehicle. No telling what we might turn up."

Casey sighed. "I need to talk it over with my lawyer first. If he's cool with it, I'll come by your office later and give you the sample."

"Why don't you call him now, and we'll wait?"

"Well...okay. Let me see if I can get him on the phone. I'll be back in a few minutes." He dropped his empty beer bottle in the trash and headed down the hall, punching in a number on his phone. When he reached his bedroom, he closed the door.

A few minutes passed, and Crook said, "Wonder how long he's gonna take. We need to get going."

"You playing tonight?"

"Yeah, a new place, and I have to set up."

Dalton went to the bedroom door and knocked. When Casey didn't answer, he twisted the knob and pushed inside. Casey wasn't there, and the window was open. A couple of coat hangers lay on the floor, and there were several on the bed. Dalton rushed back through the house.

"What's wrong?" Crook asked.

"He gave us the slip."

They went out the front door and saw his vehicle still in the driveway. "Somebody must've given him a ride," Dalton said. "Whoever it was must have picked him up down the block, since we didn't hear an engine."

"Or drove a quiet car, maybe electric."

"Why don't you take my car and drive around the block," Dalton said, handing him his keys. "See if you spot him. I'll search around the outside of the house while you're gone."

Crook agreed and headed to the vehicle.

Dalton went down one side of the house to the rear, and then back up the other side to the front. All he saw was an egret chasing a bug.

Returning a couple of minutes later, Crook said, "Somebody picked him up, and he's long gone."

They got evidence bags from the car, went back inside, and bagged Casey's empty beer bottle.

"He must be guilty," Crook said.

"Sure looks that way. I shouldn't have let him out of our sight."

"Don't kick yourself. We got the bottle. He probably didn't think about that."

A quick search inside the house provided no additional evidence. Dalton said, "If he stole anything from Gunn's safe, he took it with him. I'll drop you by your car so you can go to your gig."

"What're you gonna do?"

"I thought I'd go get a swab from Jimmy Earl."

"You sure you don't need me."

"Yeah, I'm sure. I don't expect any trouble."

After driving his partner to the office, Dalton went on to Earl's place, but didn't find him at home. Turning the car around, he headed toward Ana Kovich's house to see if there had been any activity there.

Edwards's inability to tag Casey as his attacker nagged at him. What if Casey wasn't the one? Who else could it be? His phone chimed and he glanced at the display: Tarver. "Just wanted to let you know the blood we found on the wall at the Edwards scene is a different type from his, so it definitely came from somebody else."

"That's good news. When do you think you'll get the DNA results?"

"Our courier took it to the lab and dropped it off a couple of hours ago. They said they would do their best to get us the analysis by tomorrow."

As Dalton neared the former housekeeper's duplex, his phone sounded again. He didn't recognize the number. "Hello."

"Hey, Detective, this is Colin Casey. I didn't murder anybody, but I don't want my DNA analyzed, either."

"Yeah, that's pretty obvious. Why not?"

"I have my reasons."

"Would one of them be because of the murder investigation in the U.K. that you ran out on?"

Casey paused, then said, "So, you know about that. I didn't kill that guy, but I had a fight with him an hour or two before he was murdered, and I might've left some blood on the scene."

"What was the fight about?"

"Somebody put me up to it, to try to scare the guy. I think it was the same person that put the frame on me for the murder. I had to get out of there, but I didn't kill the guy, just like I haven't killed anybody in Key West." Before Dalton could reply, he added, "I'm leaving town until you catch the guy." He hung up.

At Kovich's place, he pulled up by the cruiser on watch and lowered his window. "Anything happening?" he asked the deputy at the wheel.

"Nah. She got in her car about an hour ago, but just went down the street to the store and came back. It looked like she bought a bottle of wine."

"Okay, stay with it until you get a relief crew."

Dalton remembered Bobby Carson calling about the tattoo and headed over to his house. The old man answered the door and invited him in. He picked up a magazine and showed him the picture of the tattoo he had called about. "I'm pretty sure this is what the guy had on his right arm."

The image looked like one Dalton had seen online, but it didn't resemble the one inked on Colin Casey's arm. He snapped a photo with his phone, thanked Carson, and left. Another reason to think Casey wasn't right for the murders.

Back at the office, he took Casey's beer bottle to the CSI unit and left it with Tarver. "I don't think this is our guy, but maybe we can cross him off the list if it doesn't match the blood from Edwards's bedroom wall."

"The Edwards scene was our first lucky break," Tarver said. "We have a number of prints from his car. Maybe the attacker got careless and left his prints there. I should know more in an hour or so."

Dalton's phone chimed as he headed for his desk. It was the watch commander. "My deputies said Otto Edwards is getting released from the hospital. Do they need to take him home and stand watch?"

"Yes. His attacker might be waiting for him there. We need to keep somebody posted until he goes back to work or we find the guy."

"Okay, will do."

It was 5:30, and he wanted to wait for the print results Tarver had mentioned. Remembering the photo of the tattoo he had taken of Bobby Carson's magazine page, he brought it up on his phone and wondered who had one like it. He retrieved the videos of interviews he and Crook had conducted and started up the one for Jimmy Earl. Earl had his arms on the table in front of him, so Dalton stopped the action and zoomed in on his tattoos. There were several, but none of them were Celtic crosses. He skipped the Casey interview and moved on to the one for Sheffield and his girlfriend, Richele. A tingle buzzed the nape of Dalton's neck when he zoomed in on Sheffield's right arm. A large Celtic cross adorned most of the area between his wrist and elbow. It bore a striking resemblance to the one from Carson's magazine. Dalton brought up Sheffield's driver's license photo and printed it. He found several mug shots of men who had been arrested recently and printed them as well.

A CRUISER SAT on the street in front of Edwards's mobile home. Dalton waved at them as he got out of the car and headed to the door. Edwards answered after several knocks. "Hey, you again. What's up this time?" His eyes appeared sunken inside darkened half-moons.

"I have some more photos for you look at."

"Okay, come on in, but you need to make it quick. I gotta get in bed."

Inside, Edwards took a seat in his recliner, and Dalton sat on the end of the sofa nearest him. The wounded man took the stack of images and began flipping them, scanning for a second or two with each one. On the fourth one, he said, "I remember this guy from the jail. He was there for about a week, but he wasn't the one who attacked me." He flipped to the last page, which was Sheffield, stopped, and thumped the page with his index finger. "This could be the guy. You know how tall he is."

"He's over six feet. About your height."

Edwards nodded. "Yeah, I think it's him. His hair is a little longer now, but something about his eyes makes me think it's him."

DALTON DROVE TO Alan Sheffield's condo and found his parking space vacant. He climbed the stairs and rang the doorbell. No answer. He tried again with the same result. Nobody was stirring nearby, so he picked the lock and pushed inside. The place looked as if the owner had moved: only empty hangers filled the bedroom closets.

He found dirty glasses in the kitchen sink, and knew one of them would probably yield DNA. It wouldn't do any good, though, without a warrant. The closets and bedroom had a vacant feel, too. If he had stolen the victims' computers, he had taken them with him. There didn't seem to be anything else of value. The CSI team could give it more scrutiny when he got the warrant.

His phone chimed as he got back into his car. Crook. "Randy Teal called me about the number from Ana Kovich's phone I asked him to check. He said it belongs to Alan Sheffield, the lead guitarist for Redgunn."

Dalton told him about the tattoo and Edwards identifying Sheffield as his attacker.

"Sounds like our guy, then."

"I think so. We need to nail it down with DNA if we can." A beep indicated another call coming in, so he and Crook hung up.

When he answered, one of the deputies guarding Ana Kovich's home said, "A black Cadillac SUV just pulled in, and she ran out the door and got in. They're pulling out now. You want us to follow them?"

"Yes, but don't let them see you, and don't try to apprehend them. I have reason to believe the driver is armed and dangerous. You get the plate number?"

"Yep. I checked it out, and it belongs to a guy named Sheffield."

"Okay, stay on the line. I'm heading that way."

"Roger that. Putting you on speaker."

Dalton stuck a flasher on the roof and sped out to the highway. A minute later the deputy said, "We just turned north on A1A. A couple of cars are between us, so I don't think he realizes we're back here."

"Good, stay with them. They're probably on the run."

"You want us to radio ahead?"

"Let's hold off on that. He could have a police scanner."

"Okay, we're on them like a swarm of no-see-ums."

The cruiser was about five miles ahead on Big Coppitt Key. Dalton pushed his car as fast as traffic permitted. The sun reclined on the horizon in his rear view, casting long shadows up the highway. It would be dark within minutes, and that would make the job of tracking Sheffield more difficult.

The two deputies talked between themselves. One of them phoned the watch commander to let him know what was going on. When Dalton thought he was within a mile or so of the cruiser he shut off the roof flasher. A few minutes later the deputy said to Dalton, "Okay, they're turning onto Indies Road at Ramrod Key. It's a neighborhood, so we're dousing our headlights."

"I'm not far behind. If I remember correctly, there's water access from that road."

"Yeah, some of the houses have lighted boat docks at the rear."

"They probably have a boat waiting."

"Looks like they're turning in at a vacant lot. I'm calling for backup on the phone. We passed a sheriff's station a few minutes ago, so we should be able to get another cruiser here pretty fast."

"Tell them to come in quietly. I'm nearing Indies now." A minute later he turned in, sped along until he saw the cruiser parked on the shoulder of the road, and pulled over behind it. He got out with his Maglite.

A deputy stood next to the car. "They're down beyond those two houses on the left. Clark followed on foot so he could keep them in sight." He and Dalton hurried to the vacant lot.

The moon gave off some illumination, but it was still pretty dark. Someone had partially cleared the property, and about twenty feet in he spotted Clark on the ground, face down. They ran over to him and the deputy checked for a pulse. "He's alive. Somebody must've slugged him."

The Caddie was parked in the brush at the shore about seventy feet away, and a boat was tied there, its engine running. A dim light illuminated a crude gangplank. The boat, a trawler of about forty feet, looked like the same one that had attempted to pick up William Chan when he tried to escape. Dalton could see the silhouette of a man on board, and another man and a woman were stepping onto the gangplank. The man was wheeling a suitcase. Dalton pulled his service weapon and eased that way.

The man on the boat said, "Hey, somebody is out there."

In the dimness, the man with the suitcase appeared to turn. It was Alan Sheffield. "Get us out of here," he said, panic in his voice.

As Dalton neared the shore, the boat shoved off and Sheffield fired a shot. Dalton heard the bullet hit a cluster of palmetto a few feet away and dropped to the ground. Another shot followed, *zinging* over his head. He fired back, but the boat was already pulling away. Getting to his feet, he splashed the Maglite on the escaping craft and noted the number on the transom. The waterway was a mile-long canal, and the trawler probably had a top speed of no more than thirty mph. He ran back to his car, passing the two deputies on the way, both now on their feet and making their way toward the cruiser.

In the car he steered around the sheriff's vehicle and floored the accelerator. His tires flung sand and then screeched as they sought traction on the blacktop. The engine roared, pushing the speedometer to sixty, and then he had to brake toward the end of the road. He got out and retrieved the shotgun from the trunk. The approaching boat's motor rumbled in the distance.

He chambered a shell, ran through the side yard of a residence toward a lighted dock, and waited around the corner of a boathouse. As the boat neared, it slowed for a crook in the canal that led to the sea. Dalton aimed at the broadside of the craft near the waterline and fired. The discharge boomed in his ears, and buckshot tore a hole the size of a soccer ball in the fiberglass hull.

SEVENTEEN

THE RUPTURED BOAT took on water and listed to its starboard side, its motor struggling to maintain speed. It headed toward the far side of the canal and crashed into the seawall. The silhouettes of four figures climbed off the boat to shore and ran. Sheffield dragged a suitcase behind him. They headed along the seawall around the point toward some lighted docks.

Dalton got in his car and sped around to the other side of the canal. A couple of minutes had passed as he approached the dead end. Slowing the car, he scanned the area for any signs of the runners and thought he saw movement behind one of the homes. He stopped, exited the car, and ran toward the home's dock. As he approached, he spotted a boat pulling out from the lighted dock next door. It cruised away into darkness as he neared.

Lights flooded the yard and the home owner ran out the back door yelling, "Hey, that's my boat! Hey, stop! Stop!"

Dalton hurried over to him and flashed his badge. "I'm with the sheriff's office. Is there a boat I can use to go after them?"

The man stared, as if in shock.

"I need a boat," Dalton said.

"Yeah, okay. Munford has one next door. Maybe he'll let you use it."

"You know your boat registration number?"

He told him the number and name painted on its side and ran next door. Dalton phoned the watch commander and gave him the information.

"Okay, I'll alert the Coast Guard."

They hung up as the man ran back with a key. "Let's go after them. It's that runabout over there. It's fast, and can probably catch up to them."

"You can't go. Those guys are armed."

Without a word, the guy relinquished the key. Dalton ran to the boat and untied the lines. He keyed the ignition, backed out, and cut an arc toward the sea. Powered by two big outboards, it lifted onto a plane within seconds after he opened the throttle. The fleeing boat had headed east, which meant it would have to turn inland beyond Little Torch Key. There were lots of places along that stretch to obscure a boat and have someone pick them up in a vehicle.

A few minutes passed. Dalton hadn't spotted them, and he wondered if they had already found a secluded cove where they could hide. He kept going for another few minutes, idling along the shore of Little Torch and scanning the docks. Thirty minutes later he crossed the channel and headed back along the coast of Big Pine Key. After an hour of searching, he gave up and returned to the dock.

The man who had lost his boat stood waiting. "Any luck?"

Dalton shook his head. "They must be hiding in one

of the coves. The Coast Guard is looking for them, though. Your boat will turn up."

"I sure hope so." He didn't sound very confident.

Another man hurried down from next door. "The boat run okay?" he asked.

"Yeah it did fine, but they just had too much head-start. Thanks for letting me use it."

Dalton handed him the key and went back to where the disabled craft lay half sunken in the water. Rocks along the seawall had kept it from going under. He stretched on gloves, grabbed his Maglite, and climbed over the bow rail. After slogging through several inches of water in the salon, he found nothing of interest and went back to his car.

There were plenty of places to hide, and Sheffield would need to find a safe haven. Dalton thought about the girlfriend, Richele, and tried to remember her last name. He had it at the office, but that was more than twenty miles away. A call to Crook, who was probably playing at his club gig, yielded no answer. Then, as Dalton turned onto A1A, Crook called back.

"Hey, did you call me?"

Dalton brought him up on Sheffield and Ana Kovich fleeing in the boat. "They could be anywhere in the Gulf by now. Lots of islands to hole up there, but I was thinking he might reach out to his girlfriend for help. You remember her last name?"

"Yeah, I think it was Curtis. Richele Curtis. If you need me, I can cut out of here. The others can carry it the rest of the night."

"Let me see if I can get in touch with her. I'll call back if I need you."

They hung up and Dalton searched for the woman's phone number. When it popped up, he called, and she answered right away.

"This is Detective Michael Dalton. Have you been in contact with Alan Sheffield?" When she didn't reply, he said, "This is important. I need an answer."

"I haven't seen him since yesterday. Why are you asking?"

"He's the person who killed Riley Gunn, and now he's trying to escape. If you know where he is or where he's going, you need to tell me."

She hesitated a moment, then said, "I didn't know he killed Riley, and I don't know where he is."

When she didn't add anything else, he said, "You were his alibi for the killing. I have you on video swearing to it. If you don't come clean about that, I can only assume that you knew and maybe even helped with the murder."

"No, no. I didn't know anything about it. I was wasted when we got to the condo and passed out after another couple of drinks. He could've left, and I wouldn't have known it."

"So you lied about the alibi?"

"He told me he didn't do it. I took his word for it."

"That won't matter in court. I'll make sure you serve time if you don't help me find him. What do you know about Ana Kovich?"

"I know she and Alan are pretty thick. He said she's just a friend, but she calls him a lot."

"She might be more than a friend. He picked her up a couple of hours ago, and she's on the run with him."

She remained silent for a few moments and then

sighed. "We were at his place last night and he got a phone call. After that he acted really strange and asked me a bunch of questions about a guy I dated a few months ago."

"Who was that?"

"A man named Otto Edwards. He's a guard at the detention center. I met him when I got arrested last year on a bogus drug charge."

"What did he want to know?"

"He wanted to know where Otto lives and what it was like at the jail. I thought he was just jealous, but then he clammed up and took me home. I haven't seen him since."

"Sheffield assaulted Edwards and used his uniform and credentials to get inside the detention center. He killed a man in one of the cells."

She gasped, and then made sobbing sounds. "Is Otto okay?"

"Yes, he's going to be fine. Has Sheffield called you?"

"No, he hasn't."

"Has he ever mentioned owning any other property in Florida, maybe a rental house or a vacation home?"

She paused for few seconds, as if thinking, and then said, "I don't think so, but he did tell me about a place his grandfather owned that got taken by the bank when he died."

"Where was it?"

"Way out on Big Pine Key, on a secluded cove. He drove me out there once. It was an old house that was falling in, but he said it was pretty nice when he was young. He said he planned to buy it and fix it up."

"I need you to show me where it is."

"You mean now?"

"Yes, right now. He might've gone there. He was in a boat."

"I don't know if I can find it. I only went there with him once."

"We have to find it."

She agreed to meet him at a café on Big Pine Key in thirty minutes. It was only a few minutes away for him. He phoned the watch commander as he drove and brought him up on the boat chase. After that he called Lola Ann.

"I have a scoop for you," he said.

"What do you want?" They hadn't spoken since he declined her invitation to her place the week before. With her looks, she probably didn't get rejected very often, and apparently didn't care for it.

"Hey, is that any way to greet somebody trying to help you out?"

She sighed. "Okay, tell me what you need."

He went over the Sheffield situation. "He's on the run somewhere in the Keys. I'll send you his photo if you'll put it on the air right away."

"So he's the murderer you've been looking for?"

"Pretty sure he is."

"You'll owe me for this," Lola Ann said.

"You get to break the story. Your producers will like that."

"We'll talk about it later." She hung up.

He turned into the café lot, parked, and sent the photo.

Everything had happened since the lieutenant had

left for the day, so Dalton phoned his cell and gave him an update.

"What are you doing now?" Springer asked.

"I'm waiting at a place on A1A for Richele Curtis, Sheffield's girlfriend. She's going to take me out to a waterfront house that Sheffield's grandfather had owned on Big Pine. From what I hear, it's abandoned, and he could be holing up there."

"I'll call in backup for you."

"Thanks. I need a couple of cruisers to block the road out of the place, in case he has a vehicle. Also, can I get marine patrol over there in case he tries to escape in the stolen boat?"

"I can have cruisers there in twenty minutes, but it'll take an hour or more to get a boat up there."

"Okay, I have an idea. My uncle has a marina on Little Torch. I'll call and ask him to get a boat ready, if you can have a couple of deputies who know the waters to pick it up there."

Springer agreed and Dalton gave him the location of the marina. "Tell them to call me when they're in the water, and I'll give them the coordinates." They hung up, and he turned his ringer off and set it to vibrate. He called his uncle Eric about the boat.

"Sure, I have one they can use," Eric said. "How soon?"

"Maybe twenty minutes."

"Okay, I'll top off the tanks."

They hung up, and he went inside and had a cup of coffee and a sandwich while he waited. Richele showed up as he paid for the meal, and he went out to meet her.

"Leave your car here and ride with me," Dalton said.

As she got out, two sheriff's cruisers pulled in. He went over and told them the situation.

They took a road traveling northwest, the cruisers in tow, passing several residential areas. The houses thinned out as they neared the upper end of the key and she told him to slow down. "There's a dirt driveway here somewhere that leads out to the place. It was daytime when he brought me out here, and everything looks different now." The road came to a dead end, and she told him to turn around. He did as instructed and the cruisers followed. They rode back the way they had come until she said, "Stop here. I think this is it."

Weeds had grown over the entrance. "How far to the house from here?" he asked.

"I think it's about a hundred yards."

He pulled over to the side of the road and turned off the engine. "Okay, I want you to wait here with the deputies." He took her to one of the cruisers, put her in the back seat, and told the driver to wait there in case Sheffield came out that way. He asked the deputies in the other cruiser to go with him down the driveway. His phone buzzed in his pocket and he answered. It was the deputies on marine patrol.

"Head toward the northern tip of Big Pine," he said into the phone. "I'll send the coordinates to this number if our guy is holed up there." When he hung up, he said to the two there with him, "I think there are four of them. One is a woman. We want to take all of them alive if possible."

They drew their service weapons, and Dalton stretched a vinyl glove over the Maglite lens to diffuse the beam. He held it low to the ground as they plodded through the weeds. It would be unfortunate if they encountered a snake, because they wouldn't see it until it was too late. After a few minutes of walking, they came to a clearing. There were weeds and palmetto clusters, but fewer trees. The moonlight illuminated an old structure, facing them. Its rear would be parallel to the water. A dim light shone through a front window. Maybe a lantern.

Dalton doused his light, and they eased on toward the house. They rounded it on one side and made their way to the shore. The stolen boat sat there, tied at an old dock. He checked the GPS coordinates on his phone and sent them to the deputies on the boat. He followed up with a call. "There's only one house out this far, and a boat is tied at the dock, so I don't think you can miss it. Cut the throttle when you get close and come in as quietly as you can."

When he hung up, he told one of the deputies to cover the rear in case the occupants went out the back door. The other deputy went with Dalton as he eased around to the front porch. They each took a corner. It was deathly silent, and the faint burble of a boat's engine reached his ears, and then quieted. He called Sheffield's phone, and somebody picked up on the other end but didn't say anything.

"I know you're in the house," Dalton said. "We have you surrounded. Come out and give yourself up."

"What do you think I did?" Sheffield asked.

"You murdered Riley Gunn and a bunch of other guys. We have an eyewitness." Not exactly the truth, but close enough. Otto Edwards knew nothing of those murders, but he had identified Sheffield as his attacker, and his attacker had murdered Chan.

"Eyewitness? Who?"

"Don't worry who it is. Just do yourself a favor and come out."

The line dropped.

Less than a minute later, Dalton heard a noise from the side of the house. "Sounds like a window opening," he said to the deputy. "Keep an eye on the front door."

He peered around the side and saw two silhouettes, both men, headed away from a window toward the rear. Then a third man tumbled out. They started running toward the shore. "Stop," Dalton called, "you can't get away!"

One of the men turned and fired. Dalton fired back and saw the man drop to the ground. The other two men kept going, and then a woman joined them.

"Give it up. You don't have to die."

The woman stumbled and fell, and the two men kept going, running toward the dock. The deputy from the rear of the house rounded the corner and said, "I'll get her. Go after them."

Dalton got to the man he had shot and found no pulse. Rising, he called out to the runners, "I'm warning you. Stop or I'm going to put you down." He heard the sound of the deputies' boat engine throttle toward the shore.

One of the runners turned and fired. The bullet smacked into a tree several feet away, and Dalton returned fire, but he didn't hit home either. The runners reached their boat and scrambled aboard. The deputies on the water splashed a spotlight onto the bow of the stolen craft, illuminating both men. One of them was Sheffield. Their boat was blocked from moving forward.

Sheffield squatted below the rail and undid a tie line while the other man ran into the wheelhouse. The engine started, and Sheffield headed into the wheelhouse. Dalton raced to the rickety dock, stepped over the boat rail, and headed down the port side to the rear hatch. Certain they had already seen him, he kicked the hatch open and then leaned around the corner to peer inside. Sheffield stood next to the helmsman. He fired a shot that hit the rear hatch jamb, and wood splinters exploded next to Dalton's face. The engine revved, a gear engaged with a *clank*, and the boat lurched backward. Sheffield fell back against the console, and Dalton raced through the salon and pointed his 9mm at him. "Lay down the gun. I'm warning you."

The man at the helm cut the engine and turned to look. Sheffield got to his feet and stepped into the salon, just a few feet from Dalton. He aimed his handgun at Dalton's head. "You don't have an eyewitness. This is just a case of police harassment."

Dalton sighed. "Do what I asked, or I'm going to shoot you. I'm counting to five, and you're going to die."

"You'd shoot me in cold blood? My partner in there'll tell what you did."

"No, I'll shoot him, too. One…two…three…"

The other man ran out of the wheelhouse. Sheffield glanced that way, and Dalton stepped out and kicked his gun hand. The weapon broke loose, firing wild to the overhead, and clattered to the deck. Sheffield dived for Dalton, slamming him against the wall. Dalton kneed him in the chin. He fell back, seemingly stunned, but lunged again, and Dalton hit him in the stomach with his fist. The guitarist-turned-hit man doubled over, and Dalton kicked him in the face, putting his heel into it. Sheffield's head snapped to one side, his eyes rolled up like window shades, and his limp body dropped to the deck.

Dalton rolled him over and cuffed his wrists behind his back. After collecting the dropped handgun, he started the engine and nudged the boat back to the dock. He tied a line and strode out to see where the other man had gone. One of the deputies had him handcuffed a few feet from shore, so he disembarked and went over.

"Where's the other guy?" the deputy asked.

"He's unconscious."

"Thomas is holding the woman at the house. We'll take them and bring a cruiser down the driveway for your guy on the boat."

When he and the bound man stepped away, Dalton called Springer and told him what had happened. "We need the coroner for the dead man." He hung up, went back to the shore, and thanked the deputies on the boat. "They would've gotten away if you two hadn't blocked them in."

"Glad to help," one of them said. "Looks like you have things under control, so we're gonna head back if it's okay with you."

"Yeah, that's fine."

They backed up and cut an arc into the center of the channel headed back toward the marina. A couple of minutes later, the sound of a boat engine rumbled from somewhere in the channel. Dalton wondered if the deputies were returning, but as the boat neared, it sounded more like a powerful inboard. His pulse ratcheted up when he saw the silhouette of the craft approaching the shore. Wishing he hadn't let the deputies go, he splashed his Maglite on the approaching hull. It looked like a Cigarette boat, and there were two men aboard. The light reflected off something shiny, maybe a weapon. Dalton lunged behind a tree trunk as a man aboard fired a shot. It hit the tree, peppering the side of his face with chunks of bark. He doused the light.

The craft nudged up to the far side of the stolen boat, and a man leaped aboard. The shooter on the Cigarette fired again. It went wild, hitting a tree close by. Bracing his gun hand against the tree trunk, Dalton splashed his Maglite on him and pulled the trigger. The man fell back, and Dalton raced to the dock as a man dragged a still unconscious Sheffield across the deck of the boat. When he saw Dalton nearing, he dropped Sheffield and reached for his gun.

"Don't do it. I already shot your partner. You bring out that weapon and you'll be as dead as he is." The man stopped and seemed to consider his options, but only for a second or two. He turned, jumped onto the Cigarette, and throttled the engine. It sounded like a race car as it rose onto a plane and sped away.

EIGHTEEN

DALTON RETRIEVED SHEFFIELD'S suitcase from the stolen
boat. Inside were clothing, phones, a laptop, and a flash
drive. He took the case to his car and then followed the
cruisers to the detention center where he booked the
men, Sheffield on a murder charge, and the man who
drove the stolen boat for grand theft, aiding and abetting.
Ana Kovich was guilty of something, though he was still
unsure what, so he booked her as a co-conspirator to the
Riley Gunn murder.

On his way to the office, Lola Ann called. "You catch
my program?" she asked.

"No, I was pretty busy. You put Sheffield's picture
on the tube?"

"That's what you wanted, wasn't it? You were right:
the producer loved getting first dibs. You still owe me,
though."

"Okay, I have another one for you. We arrested Sheffield for the murder, along with two other people trying
to escape with him." He gave her some of the details.

IT WAS TWO in the morning by the time Dalton logged the
suitcase and handguns in as evidence and finished writing his report. He sent it in an email to Springer, Sheriff Diaz, Crook, and Connie Duval in the prosecutor's
office. Another email to Tarver requested a ballistics

comparison for the handguns with the rounds that killed Gunn and Hess. A few minutes later he left for home.

The marina was quiet when he got to his cottage, and sleep took him a few minutes after falling into bed. He awoke a few hours later to Cupcake purring next to his bed. It sounded like a faraway boat motor. The cat wanted his breakfast, so Dalton rose and fed him.

He went out the cottage door at ten and saw that Eric had pastries and coffee on the deck. Nodding to his uncle, who was busy talking to some guests, he picked up a cup of brew and a bear claw, and headed for his car.

"Hey, you in a hurry?" Eric asked.

Dalton stopped and turned. "I had a late night and have to get back to it."

"You get your man yet?"

"I think so. He's in a cell now."

"Who is it?" one of the guests asked.

"It'll be on the news," Dalton said.

At the office, he passed Crook sitting at his desk looking hung over. "I read your report. Guess you didn't need me after all." He sounded miffed.

Shrugging, Dalton said, "It all went down so fast, you wouldn't have had time to get there." He should have stayed around a little longer, instead of going off to play his guitar, if he was actually interested. "How'd your gig go?"

"Okay, I guess. Not many of our fans showed up. Not sure we'll go back there after this week."

Dalton just nodded, went on to his desk, and checked his email. None from Tarver. He called and asked about DNA from the Edwards scene.

"I don't have anything yet, and it should be here by now. I'll give them a call."

Dalton didn't like the sound of that. It could be a snag of some kind. "What about the prints you mentioned in the mobile home and the car?"

"Sorry, all the prints belonged to Edwards."

When they hung up, Dalton went back to his email. The sheriff had sent one asking if the prosecutor's office was on board with the arrest, so Dalton called Connie Duval.

"I read your report," Duval said. "You have hard evidence on this guy?"

"I'm waiting on DNA from the jail guard's home. As I mentioned in my report, there was blood on the wall that might belong to Sheffield."

"I figured Chan's killer was part of his distribution network."

"Well, Sheffield was a distributor, but he killed William Chan because he could finger him on the Gunn murder." He told her what had happened with the jail guard, how the Redgunn band member had slugged and drugged him. "Sheffield used Edwards's ID and uniform to gain access to the detention center so he could kill Chan."

"You said in your report that Edwards identified Sheffield from a photo. You think that's reliable after what he went through?"

"I think it's solid. He picked him out from several others."

Duval sighed. "Okay, so far it sounds iffy. You need that DNA. Gotta go. I have a court date." She hung up.

It sounded like Duval could back away without

the blood work. He prepared a warrant for Sheffield's condo, the suitcase contents, his vehicle, and a DNA swab. Within a couple of hours, he had a judge's signature on it. He got Sheffield's keys from the evidence room, and he and Crook headed out for the search. After finding nothing of value at the condo, they went back to examine the suitcase contents.

They collected the case from the evidence room, took it to Crook's desk, and checked the phones first. There were two, and neither had password protection. One belonged to Riley Gunn, the other to Wilbur Hess. Gunn's phone only reinforced what they had learned from his carrier: he had called Hess several times the night of his murder, and had called other unidentified numbers in the previous weeks. Hess's phone had lots of different numbers in its call history. Customers? Dalton suspected the numbers would be dead ends. Neither device appeared to contain any texts, documents or photos about the murders. Dalton assumed Sheffield had taken them only as a precaution, or maybe so nobody would have access to the trail of illegal drug activity.

The laptop had belonged to Gunn. It contained a spreadsheet document with entries that appeared to be drug related: dealer names, dates, drug quantities, and dollar amounts. It included Hess's name, and Crook recognized a couple of names as movers and shakers in the Key West entertainment field. There were no indications that the computer had ever been connected to the internet. It seemed of little value in identifying his murderer, but the DEA would find it interesting.

Crook plugged the flash drive from the suitcase into his computer. "I only see one file here. It's a video."

Dalton moved over to the monitor so he could watch. The video opened with a scene of an Asian woman lying on a bed, her eyes open, staring. What appeared to be blood covered the side of her face and a large spot on the bed. She lay very still, as if dead. Then the camera lens panned to Riley Gunn, who lay on the floor. His eyes were closed, and he had what appeared to be blood on his shirt and hands. Dalton said, "This must be the scene Jimmy Earl told me about that Gunn had described to him. That looks like blood, but it could have been staged. I think they wanted to get their hooks into him. He probably knew a lot of rich people who used drugs. A perfect setup for a distributor."

As if listening in, Marilyn Coe rang his cell phone. "I heard you made an arrest last night."

"That's right. Alan Sheffield. He played guitar in the Redgunn band. I'm pretty sure he killed Riley Gunn and William Chan."

"So he's the one in the video from William Chan's limo that you couldn't see?"

"Yes."

"We need to interview him."

Dalton had been bracing for that request. He knew the DEA might take Sheffield away if he couldn't produce hard evidence of his guilt for the murders.

"He's at the jail. I want to be present if you talk to him."

She paused before saying, "I'll let my supervisor know," and then hung up.

Tarver called a few minutes later. "The lab can't find the blood sample we submitted. They have it logged in, but it's missing."

Dalton wondered if sabotage might be involved. "Do they think it was just misplaced?"

"Well, they don't know. They're looking for it."

This wasn't working out as planned. "Do you have enough blood for another sample?"

Tarver sighed. "Maybe. I'll take a look." They hung up.

"Bad news?" Crook asked. He told him.

Crook said, "They could go back to the mobile home and get more, if Edwards hasn't cleaned it up."

"Yeah, good idea." He phoned Edwards and asked about the blood spatter.

"I couldn't stand all the blood." the jail guard said. "I washed it off the wall."

When he hung up, Crook must have read his face. "No dice, huh?"

"No."

Springer walked up and said to Dalton, "I read your report. Did you get the DNA you were waiting for?"

Dalton told him the situation.

"Huh. That means you don't have much on him. What, stealing a boat and resisting arrest?"

The lieutenant made it sound trivial.

"He tried to kill me."

Springer gave him a grin. Actually, more of a smirk. "Okay, his lawyer called, and he wants a meeting, right away."

"Let me guess, Douglas Vici?"

"You got it. Call him and set it up." He strode away.

"I think he wants us to be wrong," Crook said, "the way he pushed you to arrest Jimmy Earl."

Dalton just nodded and they went back to the suitcase. "What about these?" Crook said, holding a pair athletic shoes. "Didn't Tarver find tread prints from shoes like these at the rear of Blake Owen's house."

Dalton had forgotten about that. "Yeah, good catch, Buddy. We need to get them to Tarver so he can see if there's a match."

Crook took the shoes and stepped away. While he was gone, Dalton called Vici and set up the meeting for a half-hour later. He went back to his desk and read over his case notes. In the beginning, Richele gave Sheffield an alibi for the Gunn murder. She later said she couldn't say for sure whether or not he was there all night because she passed out. That didn't mean he killed Gunn. It just meant she didn't know. She later told Dalton that Sheffield had questioned her about Otto Edwards the night of the William Chan murder. Vici could probably explain that away. According to phone records, Sheffield had been in contact with Ana Kovich the night of the murder. Vici might say they were having an affair.

Dalton closed his notes feeling even worse about his case. They had to have the DNA, and that was beginning to look like a long shot.

He and Crook arrived at the detention center a few minutes early and proceeded to an interview room indicated by the jailer. Vici and Sheffield were already there, seated on the far side of the table.

The two detectives took a seat facing them, and Dalton said. "Okay, we're recording this meeting." He flipped the switch for the video to begin and described who was in attendance. "So, counselor, what do you want to talk about?"

Vici cleared his throat and said, "I wanted to let you

know that I'm preparing a wrongful arrest suit against you and the sheriff's office."

"Wrongful arrest? On what grounds?"

"Mr. Sheffield and his friends were enjoying a leisurely evening at a cabin where his grandfather had once lived. You arrived at the cabin, harassed them, and made wild accusations. When they tried to leave, attempting to avoid further harassment, you fired your weapon at them. They fired back only to defend themselves. Your charges are false, and I believe a judge will agree with me."

Dalton leaned back in his chair. He had expected as much. "We have evidence that your client attacked a detention center guard at his home, rendering him unconscious. He then dressed in the guard's uniform and used his identification card to gain access to the detention center where he murdered William Chan."

Sheffield said, "Hey, man, I didn't do that. I play guitar in a successful band. I don't attack people, and I haven't killed anybody."

Vici patted his hand. Sheffield glanced at him, took a deep breath, and didn't speak further. Smiling, the lawyer said, "What is this evidence you claim to have?"

"Blood DNA. In the course of the attack, the victim, Otto Edwards, struck Sheffield, spattering his blood on the wall. A comparison will prove your client was the attacker."

The smile still in place, Vici said, "Well, I don't believe you have that evidence. If you release Mr. Sheffield within the next hour, we will consider not filing the wrongful arrest suit."

"We also have other evidence. Inside your client's

suitcase, we found a phone, a laptop computer, and a flash drive, all of which belonged to Riley Gunn."

"Ana put those things in my suitcase," Sheffield said. "They weren't mine."

Vici nodded. "Ms. Kovich told me she took the items when she found Mr. Gunn dead. She said he gave her the combination for his safe and instructed her to clear it out if anything ever happened to him."

"I don't buy that, and no judge or jury will, either," Dalton said.

"Well, we'll see."

So, they had gotten to the former housekeeper. Maybe paid her to take the blame, promising to get her off without prison time. He had to hand it to Vici; he was pretty clever. Probably had a lot of experience helping crooks squirm out of bad situations.

"The murder charge stands," Dalton said.

"Very well. I will request a bond hearing and proceed with the lawsuit." Vici and Sheffield stood to leave.

"Hold on," Crook said. "We need a DNA swab."

The lawyer shook his head. "Sorry, you'll have to get a warrant for that."

Crook pulled the warrant from his notebook and laid it on the table.

Vici looked it over and chuckled. "Okay, take your swab. It won't do you any good."

They got the sample and a guard outside took Sheffield away.

The lawyer's apparent confidence didn't set well with Dalton. He wondered if he knew something about what had happened to the blood sample. No, that would just be paranoia edging its way into his thinking. The sample would show up. It had to.

It didn't show up. Tarver called again late in the day. The lab had apologized, but they still couldn't find the sample. Dalton headed home, the thought of sabotage again on his mind.

THE NEXT MORNING Tarver stood at Dalton's desk. "I sent a courier to the lab with the remainder of the blood. There wasn't much, but probably enough. I don't know what happened. It isn't like the lab to lose evidence. They know how important it is. What's the status of your case?"

"Sheffield has a bond hearing at ten."

Tarver shook his head. "Sorry about the delay. I'll let you know as soon as I get results from the second sample."

Dalton and Crook went to the courthouse for the hearing and sat in the back of the room. The defendant wore a suit and tie. He appeared innocent and repentant. When the judge got to Sheffield's case, Vici told him that Dalton had harassed his client, who had fired his handgun only in self-defense. "Detective Dalton has it in for Mr. Sheffield. He wants to railroad him for this crime because he can't come up with the actual murderer. The detective has yet to provide any clear evidence against Mr. Sheffield."

Connie Duval objected. "Your honor, we're not here for the trial."

The judge said, "That's correct. Mr. Vici. Do you want to request bond, or not?"

Vici gave him a solemn nod. "Yes, sorry, your honor. I got carried away."

The lawyer had made his point for the judge and Duval to hear, and was probably giggling to himself. He proceeded to argue for a small bond, claiming his client as upstanding, stable, and not a flight risk.

After a minute or so, the judge cut him off, "All right, Mr. Vici. Bond is set at $100,000." He rapped the gavel and stood to leave.

Sheffield gave Dalton a wink as they passed and went out the door. Connie Duval approached with a frown. "We have to talk." She watched as everyone filed out and then turned to Dalton. "What about what he said about you trying to railroad Sheffield because you can't find the killer?"

Dalton and Crook both denied any bias, other than what the evidence had shown. She didn't seem convinced, but nodded and began walking away. Over her shoulder, she said, "You better get the DNA."

The two detectives rode to the office in silence. When Dalton got to his desk, he got more bad news. Tarver had sent an email saying the ballistics for the gun taken from Sheffield didn't match the slugs that had killed Gunn and Hess.

THAT EVENING, DALTON had a beer on the deck with his uncle and a couple of guests. The tiki torches emitted a warm glow, and a pleasant breeze tickled his face. Eric must have sensed that he was lost in thought. He said, "I guess your case hasn't worked out."

"Not yet. Maybe it will, but at this point it doesn't seem promising."

"Yeah, you win some, and, you know the rest. Don't let it worry you. By the way I fed Cupcake. He ate a pound of meat, so he should be set for the night."

"I wondered why he wasn't out here begging for a snack."

After a few minutes of small talk, the guests drifted off to their boats. Eric stood and said he thought he would go inside. He had some things to do before bed.

"Okay," Dalton said, "you can douse the torches. I want to sit here in the dark for a while, maybe have another beer."

When his uncle had gone, Dalton got the last bottle from the cooler and popped the top. He sat there for a few minutes, thinking about what he might do to catch Sheffield in his lies, and he also thought about what Connie Duval had said. Was he biased against Sheffield? The guy hadn't even been on his radar until the evidence started piling up. First with the tattoo the old man identified, then with the calls between him and Ana Kovich on the night of the murder, and finally with the two of them trying to escape.

He took a long swallow of the beer and poured the rest out. As he stood to go inside, he heard a *crackle* noise from the woods a few feet away, like somebody stepping on a dead palm frond. Then a moonlit silhouette stepped out in the open and strode toward the deck. Dalton reached for his 9mm, but remembered leaving it and its holster in his cottage before coming out.

"Hey, Detective, you probably didn't think I knew where to find you." It was Sheffield. He held a handgun with a noise suppressor attached to its tip.

"What are you doing here?"

"I came to solve your case for you. After tonight, you won't be dogging me anymore, or anybody else, for that matter."

Dalton rested his hand on the edge of the table next to his chair. "You won't get away with it. You'll be the first person they arrest."

"I don't think so. You're gonna die tonight."

Grabbing up the table, Dalton leaped off the deck and rushed the intruder, the table out front like a shield. He felt the contact with the handgun and shoved it as hard as he could. Sheffield staggered back as the gun fired wild. Dalton dropped the table and kicked him in the stomach. The kick didn't connect as well as planned, and Dalton grabbed the gun and tried to twist if from his hand. It went off and a round hit the steel fence next to his cottage with a *zing*.

Sheffield grabbed Dalton's throat with one hand and tried to turn the weapon back on him. A flood light burst on from Eric's cottage, and Dalton heard a clanging noise at the fence behind them, and then a loud thump to the ground. The cougar slammed Sheffield to the ground. The downed man screamed at the sight of the big cat and snatched up the pistol he had dropped. Dalton grabbed one of the tiki torches and swung it, striking the weapon as it fired.

Sheffield went limp and dropped the handgun to his side.

He lay still.

Cupcake whimpered, maybe thinking playtime was over.

Dalton kicked the weapon away, peered down at his motionless attacker, and then saw blood seeping from his midsection in the area of the femoral artery. Sheffield's eyes stood wide with surprise, and he opened his mouth to speak but nothing came out. He remained that way, staring at the faraway moon.

Dalton checked for a pulse and found none. He pulled out his phone and dialed 911. When the operator answered, he identified himself, told her his location, and that there had been a shooting. "Forget about EMTs. Send the coroner and the CSIs."

NINETEEN

SPRINGER AND CROOK arrived first. Crook gave Dalton a quick smile as he and the lieutenant stepped over to the body. Not having a permit for the big cat, Dalton had put him inside the house and closed the pet door.

"What happened here?" Springer asked, his eyes narrowed.

Dalton told him, everything except the intervention of the cougar.

"So we'll find only the victim's prints on the weapon?" His tone sounded sharp.

"That's right, unless someone else handled it before he showed up here."

"All right. I'll need your weapon and badge until we get everything sorted out." Springer raised an eyebrow. "It never looks good when a dead body is found at the home of a deputy."

The CSI team entered and drove down the long driveway in their van, followed by the ME's van. Both stopped behind Springer's vehicle. When Tarver stepped over, Springer said, "Check Detective Dalton for gunshot residue before you do anything else."

Tarver did as asked and said he didn't find any. He winked at Dalton as he gave Springer the results. Dalton went inside and retrieved his service weapon and badge. He returned and handed them to Springer. "You're on desk duty until you're cleared," Springer said. "File your written statement first thing tomorrow."

"Aye, aye, Sir."

Springer gave him a dirty look, but stepped away without saying anything.

The CSI crew remained for almost two hours, taking photos, tagging and bagging the evidence, while Dr. Bragg examined the body. When he took it away in the van, everybody else followed, except Dalton. He went inside, had another beer, and went to bed. He didn't know if it was the relief of taking Sheffield off the board, or several days of sleep deprivation, but he didn't awaken for nearly eight hours.

AT THE OFFICE the next morning, Dalton wrote up his statement and sent it to all the interested parties. It was Saturday, and the place was bare. A few minutes later, the sheriff sent him an email asking him to stop by. When he arrived at his office door, Sheriff Diaz waved him in. He took a seat in one of the guest chairs.

"Congratulations," Diaz said.

"Thanks. Maybe a little premature, though."

"You still have questions?"

"All the evidence isn't in yet, but the fact that he came to my home to kill me tells me all I need to know."

Diaz nodded. "Me too. I got a report from the CSI team that only Sheffield's prints were on the gun. Springer said he has you on desk duty. Don't worry about it. We'll get this resolved on Monday. Now, get out of here and go fishing, like other people do on weekends."

BACK AT HIS DESK, the image came to mind of Douglas Vici's expression when he said he didn't think there was any DNA evidence against Sheffield. He seemed a little too confident. Dalton dialed up Daniel Crown who worked for the Florida Department of Law Enforcement.

"Hey, been a long time," Crown said.

"Yes, it has." After getting pleasantries out of the way, Dalton said, "I know it's the weekend, but I need a favor."

Crown hesitated, then said, "Okay, long as it's legal."

"We sent an important blood sample to the lab and it went missing. I think we have it covered with a second sample, but it bugs me that they might lose something like that. I wondered if you might look into it."

Crown agreed and Dalton gave him the details. "I'll drive down on Monday," Crown said, "and try to find out what happened."

"Thanks. Much appreciated."

"You bet. Least I could do after what you did for me." Some information had fallen into Dalton's lap on a previous investigation, and he had turned it over to Crown. The state agent had closed a high-profile investigation based on the information.

THE REST OF Saturday passed quickly as Dalton did repairs on the docks for Eric. Late in the day he and Eric took a skiff out to flats and channels north of the marina. They returned with several large croaker and a couple of bonefish. That night they fried the filets on the deck and invited the guests to join in for dinner. A couple of the regulars asked about the event the night before that had drawn the sheriff's vehicles and crews. Dalton downplayed it, framing it as a revenge visit that turned out badly for the visitor. When he didn't say more, the conversation turned to back to the fishing expedition that had provided dinner.

Dalton relaxed most of Sunday and took Cupcake on a long walk through the woods along the shore. The big cat stayed by his side most of the trek, but ran off a couple of times chasing egrets. Dalton was tired when they returned to the marina, and he finished the evening having beer on the deck with his uncle and the marina guests.

WHEN DALTON CHECKED his email on Monday morning, he had a message from Tarver asking him to call. "Good news," Tarver said. "We finished ballistics on the handgun that killed Sheffield. It's the same one used in the murders of Gunn and Hess. I sent the sheriff and Lieutenant Springer an email on it."

"What about the DNA?"

"I expect the results today. The lab was embarrassed over what happened to the first sample, so they said they would give the replacement top priority."

When they hung up, Dalton called Marilyn Coe.

"I heard about the guy getting shot at your place on Friday," Coe said. "Were you cleared on it?"

"Yeah, it was a no brainer. Sheffield came at me with a gun. We fought and he got the worst end of it. I never touched the weapon."

"Well, that's good to hear. So he was your murder suspect that was in jail earlier that day?"

"Yes, same guy." He told her about the spreadsheet on Riley Gunn's computer.

"Does it name names?" she asked.

"It does. Buddy recognized a couple of them as band members here in the Keys."

"Can we have the laptop?"

"No, but I'll make you a copy of the file if you want to come by and get it."

She paused, then said, "I'm still undercover, but one of our crew will drop by."

"How long are you gonna do the bartender thing?"

"Don't know. Why?"

"I hoped we could get together when all this is over."

"Okay, I'll let you know." Her tone seemed indifferent. Not exactly the response he had expected. When they hung up, he went to the evidence locker and made a copy of Gunn's spreadsheet on a flash drive.

Fifteen minutes later, DEA Agent Crandall Orr entered the office and headed to Dalton's desk. "Marilyn said you have something for me."

"Yeah, I do." Dalton retrieved the storage device and handed it to him.

"I was at her house when you called," Orr said, sounding proud of himself, like a high school kid making time with somebody else's girlfriend.

"Good for you."

"I could hear what you said to her on the phone. She's not interested in you. She just didn't want to cut off an information source."

"Okay, I'll keep that in mind."

A few minutes after Orr left, Marilyn Coe called back. "Sorry about earlier. Crandall was here, breathing down my neck. He's so jealous of you, and I wouldn't give him a second look. I'd love to go out with you whenever I can drop this gig."

"Okay, I'd hoped it was something like that. He just came in for the file, and basically told me to stay away."

"He's an idiot."

After they hung up, Crook stopped by. "You okay?"

"Sure, why do you ask?"

His partner shrugged. "Springer was pretty testy with you after what happened on Friday."

Dalton shrugged. "Water off a duck's back. I was surprised to see you there, though."

"He called while the band was on a break. They went on without me."

"Well, I was glad to see a friendly face."

His partner smiled. "Yeah, I thought you might need somebody on your side."

After an awkward beat, Dalton said, "Hey, you want to go over to the jail and talk with Ana Kovich, see if she'll shed some light on what happened with Riley Gunn?"

Crook raised an eyebrow. "You're on desk duty. You don't think it'll get you in trouble with the lieutenant."

"No, it'll be fine."

Dalton drove them to the detention center, and they asked a guard to have Kovich delivered to an interview room. When she arrived, they took seats across the table from her and turned on the video. She told Dalton she wanted her lawyer present, and he nodded. "Sure, we can do that, but first I wanted to give you some new information."

She seemed hesitant, but said, "Okay."

"We found more items belonging to Riley Gunn in the suitcase we seized from the stolen boat the night we arrested you. In a meeting yesterday with Mr. Vici and Alan Sheffield, both claimed you took the items from Gunn's safe the morning he was murdered. Vici said you were willing to confess to that." Kovich just stared without committing one way or the other. "Vici got bond for Sheffield on Friday. After he threw you to the wolves, I guess he didn't care about getting *you* bounced."

"He came to see me Friday morning. He said he will get me free of all charges."

"That didn't sound like what he told us, but it isn't important. The other thing I wanted to say, in case you haven't heard, is that Sheffield came to my home Friday night. He had a gun and said he was going to kill me. We fought, and he accidently shot himself. He died within minutes."

Tears welled in her eyes, and she sobbed. Crook went out and got tissues. When she had composed herself, Dalton said, "Since you didn't know, I gather that your lawyer hasn't been back to see you. I guess you're on your own now, since you're no longer a threat to Sheffield."

She just stared and blew her nose.

"I want to ask you some questions," Dalton continued. "We'll call Vici in if you want, but it might not be in your best interest. He'll only stonewall your case. I can make you a deal."

After seeming to consider his words, she said, "What kind of deal?"

"If you tell the truth about what happened, I might

be willing to reduce the charges against you, but only if you didn't have anything to do with Riley Gunn's death."

"I didn't know Alan was going to kill him," she blurted out. "He said he only wanted what was in the safe, and would give me enough money to go home if I could get the combination. I watched Riley open the safe one day when he was high and thought I had left the room."

"So you didn't take the items yourself?"

"No, I didn't. The only reason I gave Alan the combination was because Riley didn't do what he promised. He said if I worked for him for a year, he would pay for me to return home to Ukraine. When the year ended, he said I needed to stay another year. He paid me just enough to get by, and held my expired visa over my head. Said immigration would lock me up if they knew about it."

"Okay," Dalton said, "I understand why you would be angry about that. One thing that puzzles me, though, is that you had all that cash and Gunn's personal items when you were trying to leave town."

"Alan said the money would be safer with me until we met in Miami. He told me he would arrange a plane to Cuba, where I could get a commercial flight to Ukraine."

"Okay, one last question. I think Sheffield drove a car to a spot around the corner from Riley Gunn's home the morning he was murdered. He did it to frame Jimmy Earl, who owned the car. Did you give Sheffield a ride from that place back to his own vehicle?"

She stared for a few beats, maybe wondering if her

answer might negate any reduction in her charges, and finally said, "Yes. He called and asked me to pick him up. He said his car was stalled. I reached the place he described, and he wanted me to take him to Wilbur's house. When we got there, he asked me to take the money and things he had stolen and keep them until we could leave town. I didn't know he killed Riley. I thought he just robbed his safe." She began crying again.

LIEUTENANT SPRINGER CAUGHT them as they returned to the office. "Where've you two been?" Dalton told him. His eyes narrowed. "You're on desk duty. Do you know what that means?"

"I needed information from Kovich to close my cases."

"Buddy could've handled that." Crook just stared at Dalton, maybe wanting to say, *I told you so.* Springer continued, "I'll talk with the sheriff about this. Don't be surprised if he suspends you without pay." He stomped away.

Shrugging, Dalton went to his desk and checked email. A message from Tarver said he had results from the lab. The DNA from the blood on Otto Edward's wall matched that of the swab taken from Alan Sheffield. Tarver also wrote that the tread on the athletic shoes belonging to Sheffield matched the impressions at the rear of Blake Owen's property.

Though the findings were not a surprise, Dalton felt relief to see them in writing. He worked on his reports, getting the files ready for closure. An hour later he sent an email to all concerned parties with the following summary:

Alan Sheffield attended a party at Riley Gunn's residence, left around 2:00 a.m. and returned after 3:00 a.m. accompanied by Wilbur Hess. Sheffield shot Riley Gunn in the head and then took his phone, a laptop computer, and a large amount of cash and valuables from his safe. He and Hess left and went to Hess's home where Sheffield shot Hess in the head as well. Ballistic tests indicated that both murders were committed with the 9mm handgun later taken from Alan Sheffield.

Sheffield took Hess's phone and drove away in a vintage Camaro belonging to Jimmy Earl that Hess had stolen. He parked it in the brush around the corner from Riley Gunn's home, as if it had broken down, and left Gunn's blood inside the car to steer investigators toward Earl for the murder. Ana Kovich, Riley Gunn's housekeeper, told me she provided him with a ride back to his car. She also said she was unaware of the murder. I believed her and dropped the charge of murder conspiracy, but I did charge her with grand theft because she admitted giving Riley Gunn's safe combination to Sheffield so he could steal its contents.

I believe Sheffield also had a hand in murdering Blake Owen for William Chan. Blake was expected to testify in a case that could cost Chan millions. A witness near the crime scene saw two men walking from a vehicle toward Owen's property. One of the men had a tattoo of a cross on his arm. Sheffield had such a tattoo. He also owned shoes that matched footprint impressions taken near the rear of Owen's property. The second man involved in the murder is believed to be Charles Chan, William Chan's nephew, who was gunned down outside the federal courthouse.

Last week, William Chan, a known drug kingpin, was murdered at the detention center. Otto Edwards, a guard at the center, said a man attacked him at his home and rendered him unconscious. He later identified Alan Sheffield as his attacker. Sheffield dressed in Edwards's uniform and used his ID to gain access to the detention center where he administered a lethal dose of a drug to William Chan. He wanted Chan dead because Chan could finger him in the murder of Riley Gunn. Blood DNA accidently left on Otto Edwards's wall matched that of Alan Sheffield.

We arrested Sheffield last week. His lawyer got him out on bond, and he came to my home and tried to kill me. He died as a result of an accidental, self-inflicted, gunshot wound from his own weapon, the same weapon used to murder Riley Gunn and Wilbur Hess. I have been cleared of any culpability in his killing.

As described above, the evidence indicates that Alan Sheffield murdered Riley Gunn, Wilbur Hess, and Blake Owen. He is now dead, and I am closing those murder cases. The files are online if you want more detail.

DALTON AND CROOK headed out for lunch at a seafood shack on North Roosevelt. They took their blackened fish tacos outside to a picnic table in the shade and ate. About half-way through the meal, Crook said, "I heard Springer might be leaving."

"Oh, yeah? Where'd you hear that?"

"The sheriff's secretary. She whispered it to me in the break room a little while ago. He went in to complain about you to the boss. After a minute or two of it, the sheriff cut him off and told him he was pleased with your work. The lieutenant said, 'In that case, I want a transfer out of here.'" Crook grinned. "The sheriff told him to file the paperwork."

DANIEL CROWN CALLED the following morning. "I talked with the supervisor at the lab where your sample went missing. After doing some digging, I think it was intentionally misplaced."

"Oh yeah?"

"There were three people who would've handled the sample. As you would expect, none of them said they remembered anything out of the ordinary about it and that they followed standard procedures. I looked at security video of the parking lot the day the sample arrived. At the end of the day one of the three met somebody right outside the gate. He got in the visitor's car and stayed just a couple of minutes before getting back into his own vehicle. I suspect it was a payoff."

"Could you identify the person driving the other car?"

"Yes. According to the Florida vehicles database, the license plate belongs to a police detective in Key West named Jack Ringo."

TWENTY

DANIEL CROWN CALLED the next day with an update on Jack Ringo. "I showed him the video. At first he tried to say it wasn't him, but he was really nervous. I knew he didn't bribe the guy on his own, but he wouldn't budge when I pushed for the person who put him up to it. I told him he was going away for a long time if he didn't cooperate. He loosened up after that and gave me a name. I think you're familiar with the guy: a lawyer named Douglas Vici."

"Yes, I am," Dalton said. "He defended the murderer I told you about, and probably had Ringo in his pocket. I believe he's also the lawyer for a big drug operation in Florida." He told Crown about Eon Harbor, William and Charles Chan, and how the organization had been involved with the murder cases. "You need to talk with the DEA. They should have more information on Vici."

"Okay, great. Give me a contact, and I'll see if they're willing to play ball."

"Ringo told me William Chan offered him a security job with his company but he turned it down. I guess Vici made him a sweeter offer, or blackmailed him into making the lab sample disappear."

"Either way, he'll go to prison, but he might minimize it if he provides more details on the lawyer."

Dalton gave him Marilyn Coe's name and number

and they hung up. Word got around that Lieutenant Springer was leaving in a week for a supervisory job with the Key West PD. That came as welcome news, but Dalton thought the guy still might go out of his way in his new position to cause him some grief.

With the murders in the rear view, Dalton and Crook picked up a couple of robbery cases. They visited the places that got hit and got more details. Both were convenience stores that had security video. Though the robber wore a mask in each, the video captured his car outside the place. It appeared to be the same person in each. When they returned to the office, Crook got busy searching for the vehicle. It turned out to be stolen, so they tracked down the original owner. He had a suspect in mind: his brother-in-law. The guy had stayed with them for a few days and then disappeared. The car got taken two days later. The brother-in-law seemed to be missing, but Dalton knew they would find him.

Marilyn Coe called as Dalton prepared to leave for home. "That spreadsheet you gave us facilitated a number of arrests. We'll get twenty-three indictments in all, and I'm closing down my part of the operation."

"Hey, that's great."

"Yeah, tell me about it. I have a new respect for bartenders."

"Did you get a call from Daniel Crown?"

"Yeah. I think his angle might help us nail the lawyer." She paused, then said, "I'll be going home to Miami tomorrow. You said something about going out?"

WHEN DALTON PICKED her up, she looked different, even more beautiful than before. The purple in her hair was gone, replaced with blonde, and the butterfly tattoo had faded. They went to the Pier House restaurant, ate excellent crab cakes and salad, and made small talk. Neither seemed interested in discussing their respective cases. Dalton thought it was nice, like meeting her for the first time. When they finished the meal, she asked where he lived.

"A marina on Little Torch Key."

"That sounds nice," she said.

"It is. Very pleasant."

"I want to see it. Will you take me up there?"

At the marina they had drinks on the deck with Eric and a few guests. A gentle sea breeze filtered through the mangroves. Dalton savored the minutes: cold beer in hand, no case commandeering his thoughts, a beautiful woman nearby, the glow of tiki torches on her face. The guests discussed how nice it was to be far away from the rat race, and after a while they ambled off down the dock to their boats.

When they had gone, Eric said to Marilyn, "Did he tell you about his pet cat?"

"No, he didn't mention a pet."

Eric grinned. "His name is Cupcake."

She gave Dalton a teasing smile. "I'd never guess you'd have a pet named Cupcake."

Eric went inside and brought out the cougar. Marilyn's eyes widened as the cat neared.

"Don't worry," Eric said, "he wouldn't hurt a flea." He glanced at Dalton. "Unless you attack my nephew."

The big cat eased up to her, sniffed her hand, and gave her a big yawn. He lay down at her feet and purred.

Dalton told her about rescuing the cougar in Miami after its owner had been killed.

"I remember that case. It was in the news. So you're the one who stole him from Florida Wildlife." She gave him a smile. "I like that."

Eric wished them a good night and headed off with the big cat.

When they were alone, she said, "Well, you going to show me your cottage?"

"I thought you'd never ask."

He doused the tiki torches, and they went in and had another drink on the sofa. They kissed. It seemed to last a while, and then they headed for the bedroom, losing clothing as they went.

THE NEXT MORNING, Dalton made coffee and took her a cup. Smiling, she pulled the sheet up to her neck, rose to the side of the bed, and took a sip. "I could get used to this, if I didn't have to get back to the grind."

"You can come back anytime."

He drove her back to the mobile home where she retrieved her suitcase. She kissed him goodbye, promised to come back the following weekend, and headed north. He watched her drive away, wondering if she would return, or if her intentions might fade with the passage of days and pressures of work. One thing was certain: his attraction for her had gripped him from the moment they had met, and he wished their circumstances had been different.

On his way to the office he passed the turn for Riley Gunn's house. The rock star had died young. An old story. Fame and fortune often go hand-in-hand with tragedy and death. Gunn's story was more sinister than most. He had a drug-binged night in a Thailand hotel and it turned into something horrific; it appeared that a young woman had died at his hand. Maybe he thought he could put it behind him, but that night had sealed his fate. The dominoes tumbled, one after another, until that 9mm round slammed into his brain.

When he arrived at the office, he got a cup of coffee and sat at his desk, thinking about Marilyn: the magic of the night before, the radiance of the morning, the emptiness of her departure. Her aura played behind his eyes until Buddy Crook hurried to his desk and said they had a murder to investigate.

* * * * *